Morgan

FARRADAY COUNTRY ∼ BOOK THIRTEEN

CHRIS KENISTON

Indie House Publishing

BOOKS BY CHRIS KENISTON

Hart Land
Heather
Lily
Violet
Iris
Hyacinth
Rose
Calytrix
Zinnia
Poppy

Farraday Country
Adam
Brooks
Connor
Declan
Ethan
Finn
Grace
Hannah
Ian
Jamison
Keeping Eileen
Loving Chloe
Morgan

Aloha Series Heartwarming Edition
Aloha Texas
Almost Paradise
Mai Tai Marriage

Dive Into You
Look of Love
Love by Design
Love Walks In
Shell Game
Flirting with Paradise

Surf's Up Flirts
(Aloha Series Companions)
Shall We Dance
Love on Tap
Head Over Heels
Perfect Match
Just One Kiss
It Had to Be You

Honeymoon Series
Honeymoon for One
Honeymoon for Three
Honeymoon for Four

Other Books
By Chris Keniston

Family Secrets Novels:
Champagne Sisterhood
The Homecoming
Hope's Corner

ACKNOWLEDGMENT

This has been an interesting and challenging start to 2021. Writing a book during a pandemic had its own challenges, finishing a book during the worst freeze in a hundred years of Texas history, including no heat and burst water pipes, brought a whole new set of challenges. Frankly I have no idea how I would have pulled any of it off before the age of plug your work space into your car! Adding to it all, having my Mom in the hospital and rehab for almost a month during the final edit stage brought an even more unique dimension to the author life. Still, with all that I am delighted to see we are all still here and even though Morgan fought talking to me through this whole book, he and Valerie are here as well to share their story!

The constant support of what has clearly become my author tribe was more critical in this book than any other. Without the brainstorming lunches, online sessions, and one on one phone calls with these amazing authors, we'd still be waiting for Morgan to talk to me! Thank you, Olivia Sands, Kathy Ivan, Barb Han, Kellie Coates Gilbert and Cindy Dees. You ladies rock it!

Lastly, my daughter, who came on board to help her mother get organized in the most unorganized year possible. I love you!

CHAPTER ONE

"I'll see you one and raise you two." Eileen Farraday tossed her chips onto the table. More chips clattered, landing in the makeshift pot. Her cards had been running hot all morning. She didn't dare move. Fear of her luck changing wouldn't even allow her to run to the ladies room. Grandma Siobaughn had always said, when your blessings are running high, don't change a thing. Well, that little saying was a two-way street. Her sainted grandmother was also known to get up and walk around while playing cards in order to change her luck for the better.

"Royal Flush." Flashing a huge grin, Ruth Ann fanned her cards out and waited triumphantly for the others to show their hands.

"Blast." Sally May slammed her cards down. "Thought you were bluffing."

So did Eileen. Who knew Ruth Ann would come up with one of the few hands that could beat her four of a kind.

"Oh my." Dorothy, one of the founding members of the Tuckers Bluff Ladies Afternoon Social Club, pointed over her cards to the front door.

Tall, slender, wearing shades almost as big as her face, and a hat well-suited for a glamorous star of a 1950's motion picture, a woman stood in the doorway of the café discretely scanning the room.

The well-dressed blonde reminded Eileen of her niece-in-law Meg the day she first came to Tuckers Bluff. Too pretty and too pressed to come from anywhere around these parts. "Wonder who she is."

"New school teacher?" Abbie suggested, holding out a

coffee carafe, raising her brows at each of the ladies in silent question of more or not. "I heard she's due in town any day. Will be staying at Meg's B&B while she finds a permanent place."

"If she's the new elementary school teacher, I just celebrated my twenty-fifth birthday." Sally May skewered Abbie with a what-Kool-Aid-have-you-been-drinking glare. "No woman who works with young children on a daily basis shows up dressed like she fell off the cover of a Paris fashion magazine. Not even if she's *in* Paris."

"And especially not in dusty West Texas cattle country." Dorothy bobbed her head. "At the first sign of glue stick-y fingers or wayward Magic Marker, that woman would be running for home."

"Well, looks like we're fixing to find out." Eileen tipped her head in the direction of her niece-in-law Joanna coming through the door and greeting the newcomer. All Eileen would need was time to whip up a batch of her pumpkin brownies along with five minutes alone with Finn's wife and she'd have the whole scoop, including the stranger's blood type. *Yep. Curiosity wouldn't be killing this cat today.*

"Well, how about that." Dorothy faced the side window. "You may want to look at this, Eileen."

More interested in the newcomer, she dragged her gaze away from the two women still standing at the doorway and looked out the side window. Sitting at the edge of the parking lot, head tilted to one side, Gray, the beautiful wolf mix who now lived at the ranch, blinked at her. "What the heck is he doing all the way out here?"

"Maybe he stowed away in the back of your truck?" Ruth Ann suggested.

"Maybe." Her face pinched in thought. "But I don't think so."

"You don't suppose Gray's up to his old tricks again?" Sally May said softly.

All four heads turned to the tall blonde.

"Maybe." Eileen studied the newcomer carefully. *But for who?*

Morgan Farraday carefully watched Meg's back as she stared at the columns of two by fours that until yesterday had been the rear wall of the small family living room. This morning had been spent ripping off the sheetrock and plaster from the only thing standing between the newly enclosed back porch and what would soon be an enlarged apartment for her and Adam's growing family.

"Wow, just wow." Meg spun and flung her arms around his neck, kissed his cheek, and practically bounced away from him to once again stare at the mostly open space. "This is going to be amazing."

"It's your vision." Morgan smiled at his cousin's wife. Meg was a smart and competent businesswoman who just happened to be a heck of a nice lady—and the perfect match for his cousin Adam. The delighted, wide-eyed gaze and grin that stretched from one side of her face to the other was the best affirmation of a well-executed plan. He loved making people happy, making a homeowner's renovation dreams come true. When the homeowner was family, all the better. "Now you'll have plenty of space for all of Fiona's things."

"Tell me about it. Who knew such a little bundle would come with so much...stuff." Chuckling, she continued to look at the newly opened space instead of facing him. "When do the studs come all the way down?"

"Now."

"Really?" Hands clasped tightly closed in front of her, she spun back around, somehow smiling even brighter than a moment before.

"New support beam is in place, we don't need these anymore. Want to help?"

"You sure?"

He held back a chuckle and pulling his hammer from the metal belt loop, grinning, he extended his arm. The next thing he knew, the studs were gone, Meg stood proudly admiring the truly spacious room, and heavy footsteps sounded behind them.

"Has anyone ever told you how sexy you look in a hardhat?"

"Can't say that I have." Morgan laughed at his cousin Adam ogling his wife as if they were still newlyweds. What was it with young love and this side of the family? These two made being in love look so easy. He'd learned a long time ago that aspirations and chaos eventually won out and life—his life—was much simpler on his own.

Meg rolled her eyes, removed her hat, and handed it over to Morgan. "Thank you. That was fun."

Fun? That had to be a first. He didn't know many women who enjoyed demolition. Another place and time and Morgan would have wondered if Meg had a single sister. Even if the construction business booming and pulling him all over the state, and like now, out of state, left no time for a woman in his life, he'd learned his lesson. Fool me once, shame on you, fool me twice, shame on me. Women as special as Meg simply didn't come along every day of the week. Not without strings. Complicated strings.

Moving closer to his wife, Adam curled his arm around her waist, drew her in and gently kissed her on the lips. "Seriously, you look great and so does the room."

Meg's eyes twinkled at her husband.

The simple exchange of love and affection felt oddly personal. Morgan shifted his gaze to the fallen studs, and examined them a short while before venturing to return his attention to his cousin and the now missing wall.

Meg patted her husband's arm and turned to Morgan. "I'm so glad you suggested the wall of windows instead of the typical double framed."

Her effervescent enthusiasm shoved his discomfort aside and once again reminded him why he was glad to be here. "When you mentioned how important light is to you, it was a no brainer."

"Looking good." Ryan, his brother closest in age, came in from the hall. "Soon you won't have to keep hauling Fiona all the way out to Uncle Sean and Aunt Eileen's to avoid the construction noise."

Meg squirmed in place. "Not so sure Aunt Eileen's going to like that, even if she let Becky have Fiona for a while so she wouldn't miss out on the card game."

Ryan shook his head. "Aunt Eileen really plays poker in a café?"

"Religiously." Adam chuckled.

"Well," Ryan shrugged, smiling and shaking his head, "only a few more days and we'll be out of your hair."

The light mood that had filled the room dimmed. Ever since doing the fire rehab on Chloe's house last Christmas, Morgan had been looking for a good reason to spend more than a weekend in Tuckers Bluff. When Adam had reached out to him explaining they didn't want to move out of the B&B but really needed some more space, Morgan and his brother jumped on the chance to come and stay at the ranch in the thick of this branch of the Farradays for a bit. Maybe he and Ryan shouldn't have worked so hard and fast.

The expression on Meg's face crumpled like a Sharpei. "I'll have you know we like having you two around. Besides, I'm not so sure Aunt Eileen is going to like not having the baby every day, but she did mention that she wants to redo the master bath at the ranch. Says it's time for a walk-in shower."

"As a matter of fact," Adam waved a finger at him, "Brooks and Allison are almost ready to move forward with the next phase of the hospital."

Ryan chuckled. "Y'all wouldn't be trying to keep us in Texas, would you?"

"Yes," Adam and Meg echoed quickly.

Adam sidestepped his wife and nodded from one brother to the other. "It really has been nice having you guys around again." No doubt Adam was thinking about all the lost years between the two Farraday clans. Similar thoughts and feelings had passed over him since finding it so easy to pick up with his cousins exactly where they'd left off as teens.

"Don't look at us that way." Ryan shook his head. "It's been really great reconnecting. We'll be back more often, promise. Still, I can't shake this gnawing feeling that bringing us here to help out isn't a matter of supply and demand as much as a part of a masterful scheme of Aunt Eileen's to marry off the only remaining Farraday bachelors."

Adam coughed and Meg thumped him lightly against the arm.

"What?" Adam shrugged at his wife. "The man could be right."

Smiling, Ryan shook his head more vigorously. "I'm glad all the married Farradays are so happy, really I am, but I happen to like being single. Able to go where I want when I want. Which reminds me." He turned to Morgan. "Owen and Pax are going hunting with a few guys this weekend. Think you can finish things up here without me?"

Arms crossed, Morgan nodded. He wasn't as anxious as Ryan to hurry home. Life had been good to him. Very good. Not once in recent years had he considered something was missing in his life. Until he'd returned to Tuckers Bluff, and even though he wasn't interested in any subversive matchmaking plots his aunt might have in mind, he still liked the idea of hanging around as long as he could.

"Yoo hoo," Becky called out.

The old saying about the pitter patter of little feet was absolutely true. Morgan turned at the female voice calling from downstairs and could hear the little footsteps rushing across the hardwood floors, no doubt making a bee-line for the stairs.

"Gotcha." DJ's voice carried up the stairs, followed by the giggles of their daughter Katie, officially Caitlin Helen Farraday.

All the adults on the third floor headed downstairs. The first person to reach the bottom, Meg retrieved her little girl from her sister-in-law's arms. Fiona and Katie, being only a couple of months apart, got along like the proverbial house on fire. It was a blast to watch those two side by side explore and discover the world around them. More fun than he would have thought a few short months ago.

"We may have to reconsider putting a gate on the first floor even if it's a bit inconvenient for guests." Adam shook his head at his niece doing her best to wiggle out of her father's arms.

"Don't do it on Katie's account. We're not here enough and before you know it, she'll be running up those stairs like an Olympic athlete without supervision." DJ set his girl down, the arm of a watchful parent prepared to launch if necessary to recapture the speed demon.

Expecting her to head straight for the lower steps again, Morgan was taken by surprise when instead Katie darted in his direction and threw her arms up at him.

"Well, hi there." After a few weeks with a passel of little ones, Morgan had gotten pretty comfortable with the routine. First, he'd play *whose belly is that,* tickling her tummy, then they'd do airplane, where he'd hold her over his head and zoom her back and forth until she giggled so loud that anyone in the room laughed along with them.

Where DJ's little Caitlin was the adventurous one, Adam's Fiona was the snuggler. Always happy to tuck her head into someone's shoulder and just watch and learn from the people around her, especially her cousin. Like right now. Eventually she'd give in to curiosity and take a turn with Uncle Morgan.

"You do that really well for a bachelor." Becky's sparkling eyes remained fixed on her daughter as Morgan held her high over his head.

"I catch on quick." He pulled Katie in close and rubbed her tummy with the top of his head. Her bursts of giggles had him and every other adult chuckling too.

His cousins had indeed found the true brass ring of life. Morgan had always been surrounded by family. He and his brothers were close, very close. He'd been content with that, but now he couldn't shake the feeling that he was missing out on something really special. Of course, he'd felt that way after college when he'd gone shopping for a ring for Carolyn, and look how well that had turned out.

The hat was definitely overkill. Then again, so was the hot Texas sun. As a fair-haired kid with lily white skin growing up on the beaches of Southern California, it hadn't taken Valerie Moore long to learn the sun was definitely not on her side. Overstatement or not, hats were her friend.

"Valerie?" A petite, dark-haired woman with a smile as bright as the Texas sun looked up at her.

"Joanna?"

The woman stuck her hand out. "Welcome to Tuckers Bluff."

"Thank you." So far so good. Joanna was as pleasant in person as on the phone.

A waitress sidled up to Joanna sporting an equally bright grin. Coming from California, there was nothing unusual about everybody around you smiling, but these people all looked like Cheshire cats. Maybe it was the Texas heat.

"Well, this is a nice surprise." The waitress offered a quick hug.

"Hey." Jo returned the familiar embrace, turned and waved her arm to Val. "Valerie, this is my cousin-in-law, Abbie."

"Nice to meet you." Abbie nodded.

"Pleasure," she responded, trying to add a little more oomph to her own smile.

"Since I'm in town, thought I might pop in later and visit with Brendan—and Jamie too, of course."

"Of course." The woman laughed. "If you go, make sure to check if he's home or taken the baby to the pub, though it's harder for Jamie to work now that Brendan is crawling."

Baby? At the pub? Val's gaze shifted from one woman to the other. Surely there had to be a good reason for a baby at a pub. Nothing came quickly to mind but she figured it had to be a doozy and then wondered if it was crazy enough to spin into a sitcom? Mentally shaking her head, she took a deep breath. Nobody liked a desperate producer. Too bad, the potential antics were starting to play in her head like a movie reel in fast motion.

"Everything okay?" Joanna asked her.

"What? Yes. Why?"

"You're shaking your head."

"Oh." Val laughed. Her expressions and gestures gave her thoughts away a few times too many. "Sorry, was thinking too hard."

"Ah." Joanna flashed that blinding Texas smile again.

"Table or booth?" Abbie grabbed a single menu.

"Booth. In the back."

"Got it." Joanna's cousin nodded and led them to a corner booth with a bit of distance between them and the nearest table, and handed Val a menu. "Things shouldn't get crowded for about another hour."

"Thanks."

It took a few moments to order drinks, establish that Joanna, and just about everyone else in town, didn't need a menu, and settle into their seats before her phone buzzed and anticipation zinged through her system. "I have to take this. Will you excuse me?"

"Of course."

Weaving her way through the tables to the back hall in search of privacy, she passed a freestanding ladder, briefly considering who leaves an empty ladder in the middle of a hall. Phone to her ear, she debated ducking into the ladies room, but the way her luck had been running, every stall would be occupied and all would echo loudly when flushed at the same time. Turning her back to the dining area, she jammed a finger in her other ear and buried her face in the dark corner. "What did they say?"

Her best friend since freshman year at UCLA, and a screenwriter for one of the hottest serial adaptations on cable, Marilyn had used her connections to pitch this last idea. The hope had been that Val's efforts might get farther with an insider in her corner. "No go."

Crud. That's what she was afraid of. Her forehead thumped against the hard wall. Three series pitched, three series struck out. She couldn't blame them, she wasn't all that enthusiastic about the last project either, but getting out of the reality TV game was her best shot at a new full-time gig and moving her career to the next level. Too bad no one else thought so.

"You still there?"

"Yes."

"Sorry. Switching gears in this industry isn't easy."

Brother, did she know that. The question now was, even if she convinced Joanna to give her an option on the new book, if she couldn't get backing for anything but reality TV, what did it matter how good a story she brought to the table.

"They'd be interested if you come up with a fresh concept for a new home renovation show."

And again, wasn't that the problem? How many ways could a producer spin a married couple, any couple, fixing up old houses?

"That TV home remodel with all those retro stars was a hit. Maybe we should try something like that?"

"Then it wouldn't be fresh, would it?"

"This is Hollywood. Fake it."

"Easier said than done." If only she could fake her dwindling bank account. Lifting her head, she blew out a long, slow breath. "I'm at lunch. Let's talk later."

"Sounds good. Call when you get back to LA."

"Will do." Squeezing her eyes shut, she said a silent prayer. Her gut told her Joanna Farraday's book held the answer to all her problems.

Eyes open, she spun around, surprised by the blinding burst of light from a distant window. Taking a short step, she blinked and took another before her toe connected with something clunky. Her gaze dropped to the ground, still struggling to make out what was right in front of her. Who moved the ladder?

"Sorry." The voice was deep and low and very male.

Her gaze lifted. "No prob…" The words dried up in her mouth. Teetering on that once empty ladder, directly in her line of vision, perfectly rounded denim-clad masculine buns of steel came into *very* clear view. One muscular leg descended a step, pulling the denim more tightly against said steel buns. If she could have conjured up a drop of saliva she would have whistled.

"Excuse me," he rumbled.

Slowly her gaze dropped to his leather boot and back to that well-formed derriere and up to a state sized belt buckle.

"I need to get down."

Down? Once again, her focus wandered up and down before her brain finally began to fire on all pistons, realizing she was standing in his way. Taking a step back, her mouth connected with her brain. "I'm sorry. I didn't hear you come in."

"You were on the phone. It seemed important, but I only had a couple of minutes and I promised Abbie I'd take a look at the light."

"Yes." The single syllable wasn't quite the appropriate response, but the almost hypnotic timbre of his voice had veered her mind off track again. Stringing coherent words together wasn't going to happen.

On the ground, he slid a screwdriver into a pouch that hung from his hip. The way his hand rose to his forehead, she almost thought he was about to tip a nonexistent hat. "Thanks. Have a nice day."

A smile spread across his face, her gaze leveled with deep twinkling blue eyes, and for the second time in only a few short moments, her mouth went perfectly dry. Somehow she managed to mumble, *you too*, as he lifted the folded ladder and turned to walk away. The hammer and who knows what else jingled with every step he took. No wonder the network wanted a fixer upper show. She could binge watch that man at work any day.

CHAPTER TWO

"Light's all fixed. The ballast was loose." Morgan slid the ladder into the storage closet.

"Thanks. I really appreciate it." Abbie held out a dish with a slice of Frank's Dutch apple pie.

"No time. Ryan is heading home this afternoon. I'll be finishing up Adam and Meg's on my own."

"I still can't believe how much just the two of you have accomplished in a short time. We could have used you when Brooks and Allison were turning that old mansion into a hospital."

Had he and his brothers known, they would have gladly made room for a project like that. Not only had it involved family, but he understood how important good health facilities were for rural areas. Even though Tuckers Bluff had grown a ton since he was a kid, the town was still surrounded by an awful lot of nothing West Texas. And cows. "I'd better get a move on it."

"Well, at least let me wrap the pie up to go. Maybe throw in a little bit of today's meatloaf."

Morgan shook his head. "I'll pass on the meatloaf. Meg already put out a lunch spread suitable for a king, but I might be able to sneak in an afternoon snack of apple pie."

How such a deep down rumble of laughter erupted from such a petite woman, he didn't know, but Abbie's simple amusement made him laugh too. It was one of the things he loved about being with this branch of the Farradays. As much as he loved his mom, her nature tended toward the serious side. She simply didn't seem to have that inner joy that was so easily found at every turn of his day here in Texas.

He'd managed to make it halfway to the front door with only having to wave goodbye at his aunt rather than pause for a proper good-bye. The woman took her poker seriously. Besides, it wasn't like he wouldn't see her at the ranch tonight for dinner. He glanced to his left before reaching for the door handle and spotted the striking blonde from the hallway. Just as when her eyes lifted to meet his earlier, his gut tightened, his heart seemed to trip over itself, and his brain reminded him that was exactly the type of woman with high aspirations that led to complications he didn't need.

The striking blonde was lunching with his cousin Finn's wife. His body twisted, shifting his center of gravity and reprogramming the direction of his steps. He set one foot in front of him before his brain shouted at him once again. No matter how intriguing his reaction to the stranger was, he had work to do, and that left no room for tangling with a woman.

"Forget something?" Abbie stood beside him.

"No." He shook his gaze free of the woman whose name he didn't even know. "For a moment I thought maybe, but no. Catch you later."

He'd made it outside and to the truck before giving in to the urge to look back. Hand on the top edge of the driver side door; he glanced up to the café window. Too bad he'd lost his appetite for complications. They just weren't worth the risks.

It had taken everything in Valerie not to search the restaurant for the handsome electrician.

Joanna gestured around the eatery with her hand. "I know it doesn't look like much, but trust me the food is delicious."

"I'm sure." She had indeed eaten in enough small-town places along the California coast to know appearances weren't everything when it came to food, but her mind was still kicking around her reaction to that man, not paying any attention to the menu.

"Who would think that a grumpy former Marine could make a killer Irish stew."

Marine? Didn't they only eat canned foods and chipped beef?

"Don't look so startled. The man does magic with meatloaf."

"I think I'll have an easy cobb salad." She set the menu down and moved forward with her plan. "As I mentioned in my emails, I was given an advanced copy of your new book, and I truly enjoy your voice."

"Yes. Thank you. I was a little nervous shifting from historical fiction to contemporary."

"Don't be. Some people are good writers, some are good storytellers, and you are both. And you've proven you can straddle two completely different times in history."

"Both were lots of fun to write. Are you planning on visiting the ghost town while you're here?

"If I have time." Sadly, time seemed to be one thing she had plenty of at the moment, which is why she needed to get back to the option. "Series are very popular."

Joanna nodded.

"I think your book could be expanded to work for television or the big screen."

Joanna's mouth dropped open, snapping shut at the thunderous sound of crashing metal on metal that echoed from the kitchen. Abbie, who had only been a few feet away, bolted through the double doors. Across the café chairs scraped loudly on the tile floor as four older women hurried after the owner.

"That didn't sound good." Valerie kept her eyes on the kitchen doors.

"It sounded worse." Halfway out of the booth, Joanna had one foot on the floor ready to bolt when the double doors flung open.

Abbie came through waving her arms. "Sorry about the noise, folks. Everybody take a seat. I'll be right with you."

"Well, I suppose that's a good sign, but I wonder what

the heck that was." The way her lips pressed tightly together and she fidgeted in place, Joanna seemed to have pushed aside any thoughts of books or screen rights and looked anxious to go and check things out for herself.

"If you'd like to see what's…" Valerie's words fell off as an attractive older woman in jeans and cowboy boots scooted up to the table.

"We have no idea why, but Abbie's new shelving system that holds all her pots and pans and most of the dishes came crashing down. Thank heaven no one was standing there at the time."

"Oh, good grief." Joanna shifted in place. "I've been in there. That's a ginormous shelf."

"Chock full of huge pots, too. The place looks like a bomb went off. The impact actually knocked things off other shelves. It's a terrible mess," the other woman added before even noticing Val was seated with Joanna. "I'm sorry. I'm Eileen Farraday."

"Valerie Moore."

"Where are my manners?" Joanna shook her head. "This is my husband's aunt."

"Don't stress over it." Eileen patted her niece-in-law's arm. "I called Morgan quickly. He was only a little ways down Main Street. He's turning around to come back. I'd better go help straighten out the mess so he can secure the shelf the right way. See you later."

Before anyone could say a word, Joanna's aunt had spun about and came short of breaking into a full-on run to the kitchen.

"Do you want to go help? We can chat later."

"I do, but I'm not going to." Joanna reached for her drink.

"Are you sure?"

Glass in hand, Joanna nodded. "I wouldn't be surprised if Aunt Eileen didn't have everything in order long before Morgan arrives."

The old fashioned bell over the doorway sounded and with one glimpse of the tall denim-clad Texan, it suddenly struck Valerie who Morgan was. "The electrician."

"That's my husband's cousin from Oklahoma, Morgan. I suppose he does electrical. He and his brothers are contractors. Well," Joanna shrugged a shoulder, "at least he, Ryan and Quinn are. I think some of the other brothers are on the business end of the construction company."

Construction company? An idea was starting to form in the back of her mind. If the other brothers looked like Morgan, possibilities for something fresh were beginning to take root. A whole crew of handsome men in cowboy hats could easily make rehabbing a chicken coup seem like fascinating television watching.

Once again, the bell rang by the door and as sure as her name was Valerie Moore, she was convinced the good looking guy in jeans, a cowboy hat, and a deep frown, hurrying into the kitchen had to be one of the other Oklahoma construction cousins. *Construction Cousins.* Oh, if the third brother fit the same family mold, she'd just hit the reality television show trifecta. While brothers flipping houses wasn't exactly a fresh concept, if two were a good thing, three had to be better. Didn't it?

"Anyhow, to answer your question, I have considered doing a second book on Sadieville and its decline to a ghost town."

Ghost town. A light flickered in her addled brain and her gaze drifted back to the closed doors the two men had raced through only minutes ago. Details were falling into place like a line of dominos. Her gut had been right about Joanna, just the wrong book. She'd still want an option for the contemporary that would make a great TV family saga, or movie, but gold for her was in these cousins and the ghost town. The network big shots and their deep pocket investors were right about one thing. When it came to reality TV, she knew her stuff and could smell a winner from a mile away. Like it or not, it was time to accept this side of the business was where she belonged. That popular retro TV show may have remodeled a famous house, but how many producers had pitched having three hunks bring an old ghost town, or what was left of it, back to life?

"I thought you were heading home?" Taking in the layer of pots and pans and assorted cooking utensils scattered across the kitchen floor, Morgan turned to face his brother.

"I was just about to head out when I heard there was a problem." Ryan's gaze quickly ran over the same mess Morgan had scanned and now the two studied the torn up wall.

Sticking a finger in one of the large holes near the ripped sheetrock, Morgan pulled out a dangling piece of shredded plastic.

"What's going on?" Out of breath, Jamie rushed through the doors. Eyes bright with concern darted about the kitchen.

There was little doubt in his mind what Jamie was searching for. Morgan waved his thumb over his shoulder toward the back door. "Your wife just stepped outside with Aunt Eileen to bring in some trash cans."

Relief instantly washed over Jamie. "All I heard is there was an emergency at the café. What the heck happened?"

Morgan held out his hand. "Whoever attached the shelves intended to hold hundreds of pounds of professional kitchen equipment didn't think finding a stud was necessary. The wall gave up."

"Lord love a duck." Jamie shook his head and leaned over to pick up a pan from the ground and set it on a pile that was started to one side. "Even I know you don't use plastic anchors for anything this heavy."

"I'll head back to Meg's and grab some sheetrock to patch the wall." Morgan slapped his hands together. "Abbie's going to need her kitchen back."

"We'd better get started." Ryan pulled at a torn piece of hanging sheetrock.

"No." Morgan waved an arm at the bag of debris Aunt Eileen had already swept aside. "We've got plenty of help. You go on home as planned. Give Mom a hug from me."

Ryan hesitated, his gaze bouncing from the tattered wall

to the mess all around him.

"Go," Morgan repeated.

"He's right." Jamie nodded. "I handed Brendan off to Joanna. Let me get him and drop him off at Meg's then I'll be back to come help."

"See?" Morgan waved at his brother. "Go. We've got this covered."

Lips pressed tightly in a thin line, indecision was clearly painted on Ryan's face.

"Here we go." Aunt Eileen came through the rear doorway, lugging a large gray trash bin. "We'll have the debris cleared up in no time."

"I've got another." Abbie followed in her aunt's footsteps. "And a box of heavy duty black bags."

As if he hadn't seen his wife in a month of Sundays, Jamie scooted around his aunt and scooped his wife into a tight embrace.

Abbie smacked him playfully on his hip and pulled away. "It was a shelf—not the roof—and I wasn't anywhere nearby when it fell."

"Doesn't matter. You, or the wall, still scared the hell out of me."

Abbie smiled sweetly and kissed her husband's cheek.

"I need to get a few things from my truck." Morgan bit back a smile of his own. Definitely some kind of love bug in Tuckers Bluff. "I'll ask Joanna if she can take Brendan over to Meg and Adam's instead so you can get started."

Already bending over and chucking debris into the can, Aunt Eileen called over her shoulder. "Good idea. The sooner we get this straightened up the better. And you," she turned to Abbie, "go back to handling the customers. Jamie, if you'll take over here, I'll hit the storeroom and see if I can find the right paint color for when Morgan patches the wall. By tomorrow morning no one will know what happened."

Like recruits following orders, everyone nodded and disbursed. He'd only served a few years in the Corps, but long enough to know his aunt would have made one heck of a drill sergeant. He had no doubt she'd be the kind of leader whose troops would march into hell and back for her. And why not? Not a single member of the Farraday clan, himself included, wouldn't do the same.

At the other end of the café, Joanna was up on her feet, a toddling little boy gripping one finger of each of her hands waddled a slow step at a time in front of her. Judging by the huge grin on her face, she was enjoying the little stroll as much as the adventurous little boy.

Not far behind her, the blonde stood watching the two. Her smile was wide and sparkling, and made her eyes twinkle with something he couldn't quite put his finger on, but whatever it was, it made her seem much happier than she had in the hallway.

Ryan's voice rang clearly across the café. "Didn't expect to see you here."

Neither had Morgan. He assumed Neil would be going on the weekend trek with his other siblings. Rather than catch up to Joanna, he veered right toward his brothers.

"I guess you're not joining the guys this weekend?" Ryan already had one hand on the front door handle ready to make his escape.

Hat in his hand, their brother Neil shook his head. "Heck no. With all of you armed and shooting, I figure I'd be safer in Texas."

"You can say that again." Morgan slapped his youngest brother on the back. Ryan was actually an excellent shot, all the brothers were, but at a hormonal thirteen years of age, Ryan had suffered the misfortune of letting the sight of Mary Lou Keller in her new bikini distract him. Instead of emptying the chamber when putting away his gun, he'd put a hole in the water heater and flooded the ground floor. Of course Ryan would be old and toothless some day and his brothers would make sure he never forgot. "Besides, I wouldn't object to an extra pair of hands."

Neil nodded. "I figured as much. As soon as I heard Ryan was coming home for the weekend, my coming to visit for a few days seemed like a pretty good idea."

"Neither one of us figured on Abbie's kitchen shelves falling over and bringing most of the wall with it."

Eyes rounded, Neil's chin lifted, pointing in the direction of the kitchen doors. "Anyone hurt?"

"Nah." Morgan shook his head. "Just a few dented pots."

Just then the kitchen door swung open wide and shoving her long sleeve up one forearm, and then crossing to do the same with the other, Aunt Eileen brushed dust from her hands before waving them at her nephews in a hurry up shooing motion, and then, without a word, turned and stomped back into the kitchen.

"Looks like Aunt Eileen is in drill sergeant mode." Neil hung his hat on the nearest hook.

"Say hello to Uncle Morgan," Joanna coaxed Brendan. Coming to a stop at Morgan's feet, the little boy threw his arms up.

"Nice to see you partner." Morgan was all set to tickle the baby when Brendan spotted Neil and flung himself in his uncle's direction so hard Morgan almost lost his grip. Toddlers sure came with an awful lot of momentum.

"Whoa, partner," Neil huffed as he caught the energetic little boy.

Brendan put a flat palmed hand on both of Neil's cheeks and began to pat and giggle. Another second and his uncle's face forgotten, Brendan was equally absorbed in the striking blonde female face captivated by the interaction.

Morgan had to hand the kid one thing, he certainly had good taste.

CHAPTER THREE

Oh, how lucky could a girl get? Valerie nearly squealed with delight when the handsome cowboy who caught her eye turned out to be another Farraday. So all three brothers were hunks. That barometer in her gut that always came to life when a brilliant idea was taking form had gone from measuring keen possibilities to screaming blockbuster probability.

The toddling nephew threw his arms at her, and so engrossed in the thoughts rattling around in her mind, she almost didn't catch him. "Oh, you are a handful."

"Sorry about that." Tilting Brendan upright and fully into his own grasp, the third brother flashed a mind-numbing smile. "I'm Neil Farraday. Excuse this fellow's brazenness. He clearly has good taste."

"Valerie Moore. No apologies necessary. The attraction is mutual." She held her arms out, and with a big grin connecting chubby cheeks, little Brendan flung himself once again in her direction.

The sound of a definitely male voice clearing his throat drew her attention away from the baby boy.

"We haven't been properly introduced. I'm Morgan Farraday."

The timbre of his voice sent tingles to her toes. She imagined if warm thick honey had a sound it would be this man's voice. "Nice to meet you. Again."

A soft, lazy smile centered a dimple on each cheek. Grin firmly in place, Morgan turned to face Joanna. "Jamie was wondering if you would mind taking Brendan over to Meg's to play so Jamie can help with the clean up."

Joanna pressed her lips tightly together and whispered,

"I'm in the middle of—"

The baby cooed merrily in Valerie's arms and grinning, she turned to Joanna. "We can finish our conversation later on. I'd be happy to help entertain this fellow."

"We could go to the park," Joanna suggested.

Brendan turned and frowned at her as if he'd understood the conversation and objected to her plans.

"Or not." Joanna laughed.

"Or not," Valerie agreed. "I think he likes all the people here."

"If you've got this," Morgan took a half step back, "I've got to run to the B&B and pick up some material."

Shucking out of his jacket, Neil rolled up his sleeves. "I'm ready to start pitching in."

"You're in construction as well?" Valerie was counting her lucky stars until Neil shook his head.

"Not exactly."

Morgan waved a thumb at his brother. "He's the pencil pushing end of the business."

"Accountant?" Valerie wondered if there was any way to spin accounting into dreamy.

"Architect. I do all the design work, but don't mind getting my hands dirty."

Already two steps closer to the front door, Morgan skewered his brother with an impatient glare. "Planning on handing out resumes?"

"No." Neil winked at Valerie and hurried off behind Morgan. "Talk to you later."

There was no denying those were two fine looking men. Especially her electrician. The pencil pusher had a killer smile that could make any woman lose her trend of thought, but something about the electrician drew her in and wouldn't let go. Clearly all the brothers were cast from the same mold. Tall, dark and dreamy. All good things for reality television stars. And if the rest of the pieces to her idea fell into place easily, her career was about to get a whole lot better. Shifting the baby higher on her hip, she faced Joanna. "Tell me more about this ghost town."

"No one would ever know that just a few hours ago this kitchen looked like a war zone." Hands on her hips, Abbie nodded her approval.

"Paint is still damp, but we didn't want to wait till morning to install the shelving." Morgan wiped his hands on an old rag and shoved it in his back pocket. "Now all that's left is to clear this stuff off the floor before someone trips over a stockpot and breaks their neck."

"We can handle that." Frank the cook set a plate with his popular meatloaf dinner on the shelf for the waitress to pick up, and stepped away from the stove. "I've been meaning to rearrange that shelf ever since it was installed and there's no time like the present to take care of it. I think Abbie would agree with me if I said you guys deserve a tall beer."

A nice cold beer after a hard days work was a definite perk to visiting with their Texas family. After all, no one in Oklahoma owned an Irish pub. "You sure?"

"Positive." Frank slapped Morgan on the back and waved an arm toward Neil cleaning up some tools by the slop sink. "You guys have done your part."

Standing with the stack of dinner plates in her arms, Abbie crossed the kitchen to set them on the shelf.

"That goes for you too." Frank moved the pile to a new spot on a different shelf. "It's quitting time for all of you. Donna has been here for 20 minutes. All of you, get out of my kitchen."

Morgan had the unexpected impulse to salute the cook. Instead he settled for a simple "yes sir."

"What did I tell you about calling me sir? I ain't no officer."

Abbie winced silently, and Neil shook his head. Morgan knew better, but some habits were hard to break.

"Come on guys, he's right. Finn probably has a couple of pub chairs with your names on it and I have a little boy waiting for his mama. Let's get out of here."

It hadn't taken long to pack up the last of their tools and agree it made no sense at this hour to head over to the B&B, so a quick beer before heading out to the ranch it would be. And apparently they weren't the only ones with that idea. In a back corner with barely enough light to see your own nose, Aunt Eileen and the ladies afternoon social club had set up another poker game.

"There you are." Aunt Eileen waved them over. "One last hand, then we'll be on our way home. I've got a pot roast in the slow cooker."

Of its own rude volition, Morgan's stomach rumbled. Not till the words pot roast were mentioned did he realize how hungry he was, nor did he remember that he had skipped lunch.

As Morgan and his brother pulled out a couple of chairs at the table next to their aunt, Jamie set two beers down in front of them. "I can't tell you how much I appreciate what y'all did today."

"You make it sound like we single-handedly built Rome in a day." Neil snagged the longneck beer bottle and tipped it at his cousin. "Thanks."

"You might as well have. You don't know what it was like rehabbing this place on something close to a schedule. If you two weren't in town, we would have done it ourselves. It would have gotten done," he stared at them pointedly, "but not as fast or as well as you guys did it."

"You're welcome." Morgan tipped his beer bottle at his cousin with the same gesture of thanks his brother had.

From the opposite side of the pub, Joanna exited the hallway. A time or two this afternoon on his way to get something from his car, Morgan had noticed Joanna and her friend were still at the café. The last time he stepped outside to ask Abbie about the paint, he noticed they were gone and couldn't help wishing it hadn't been such a hectic day. When the blonde woman had bumped into his ladder he'd been slightly disgruntled at her not seeing him. After all, how does a person not notice a six foot ladder with a six foot man standing on it? By the time his gaze landed on her, disgruntled was the last thing he'd felt.

"Who knew a ten month old could have so much energy?" Joanna collapsed in the seat beside him.

His gaze drifted to the hall, anticipating another person following his cousin-in-law, and hoped the disappointment didn't show when he gave up and turned back to Joanna.

"I mean, it's not like I haven't spent time with all the little ones, but usually it's just for a few minutes here and there. Half hour tops. I don't know how people do this all day every day for…"

"A couple of decades," Neil filled in.

"Well." Joanna reached for a cola Jamie had dropped off. "I don't think even the most devoted mother would be that attached to her child for that long."

"Not according to my mother." Neil shrugged. "Small children little worries, big children big worries. She went from worrying if we'd fall down learning to walk, get hurt playing football, meet the wrong kind of girl in college, or find the right wife. She likes keeping tabs on her sons no matter how old, though by now she's probably willing to marry us off to a Lucrezia Borgia wannabe if it meant she'd get grandchildren."

"Yep." Morgan agreed. That pretty much summed his mother up in a nutshell. The woman was a perpetual worrier. She would miss the sweet scent of a rose worrying about a thorn. Roses brought his mind back to the blonde. His gaze drifted over to the hall and back.

"Don't you think?" Joanna stared at him, expecting a response to something, but what?

Neil shook his head and chuckled. "Don't mind him, he has the attention span of a gnat."

"I do not."

"Okay fine." Neil sat his bottle down on the table. "What do you think then?"

Morgan really hated when one of his kid brothers got the best of him. He turned to Joanna. "I'm sorry. What?"

Lips pressed tightly together, she giggled momentarily. "Revitalizing Three Corners."

Oh, he really must have missed a good chunk of conversation because he had no idea, even with the hint, what she was talking about.

A beacon of daylight shivered through the open pub door, and Joanna sat up straighter. "Here she is. She can tell you more about it."

Morgan and Neil both pushed to their feet.

"Please," Valerie smiled, "sit back down."

Both Neil and Morgan grabbed the back of the chair between them. Morgan tugged a fraction harder than his brother and gestured with his free hand for Valerie to take a seat between them.

Chairs scraped against the hardwood floors as Aunt Eileen and her friends pushed away from the table. Collecting their plastic winnings, the women hugged and talked, and one by one waved goodbye and made their way out of the building. Aunt Eileen stopped at the table and dragged a nearby chair closer. "Nice to see you again. Valerie, isn't it?"

"Yes." The woman smiled.

"Joanna was telling us you have a new idea?"

"I do." Valerie leaned forward in her chair and faced Morgan and his brother. "And it involves both of you."

Back in her room she'd done a little research on the former town of Three Corners. The only current record of ownership was one property to a limited liability corporation, Sisters' Parlor, and as far as Val could tell, the rest of the town belonged to no one.

"Ever watch any of the fixer upper shows on television?"

Joanna groaned. Somewhere between babysitting and French fries, Joanna had mentioned her maiden name was the same as the popular home remodel television show host and the occasional challenges it had brought her.

"Sorry." Val flashed an apologetic smile.

"Mom loves those shows," Neil offered, but neither of the brothers seemed to react much beyond that. "But what does this have to do with us?"

"Well." She debated laying all her cards on the line now or perhaps the drip method of information might be more successful. "They're very popular. I'm a television producer of reality shows and I have networks wanting me to do a new home reno show."

All pairs of eyes remained fixed expectantly on her.

"I want to rebuild Three Corners." She leaned back in her chair and waited for the response.

The only person to perk up was Eileen. "Really? Rebuild as in restoration or a new Vegas strip?"

"While a new Las Vegas has some great potential, I only produce rehab shows."

"Ooh!" Eileen slapped her hands together. "This could be fun."

"And that," Valerie pointed at Joanna's aunt, "is the reaction I'm hoping to get. But before I pitch it, I could really use a bit of professional input. After all, many an old structure—and the money invested—could come tumbling down with a strong wind."

"Not Sadieville." Referring to the town's once popular nickname, Jamie stopped at the table to check for empties. "That place is solid. I helped the sisters do some sprucing up at the Parlor and it surprised the heck out of me that termites hadn't taken up residence and turned the place to dust."

Morgan's head turned ever so slightly. The wary look in his eyes was not a good sign. Obviously the drip was going to have to come very slowly.

"I'll have to come up with some catchy title for the show, but the gist of it is, bringing a ghost town back to life." She'd mention the sexy cousin contractors later. "I want to talk to the sisters that own the Parlor House."

"That will be easy. Not only is the boutique just down Main Street, Sister and Sissy love chatting up new people." Eileen nodded.

"Sister and Sissy?" This town was the gift that didn't stop giving. She really did need to meet these two women and see if they were as intriguing as their names. After all, quirky characters made TV shows hits. "But going to see the ghost town is my first step. Are you free to play tour guide tomorrow?" She looked at Joanna.

The woman shook her head. "Not tomorrow. I have back to back video conferences scheduled starting at noon."

Val swiveled around to the two contractors who didn't know yet that they were about to become television stars. "That's okay. What I absolutely have to have, though, is a professional assessment. From licensed contractors."

Neil was the first to shake his head. Lips drawn in a thin line, Morgan slowly shook his head. "I have to get Meg and Adam's place done. Sorry."

A phone rang and Eileen turned away from the table. "Hello. Oh hi." Her forehead wrinkled and she looked to Morgan. "It's Meg. She said you're not answering your phone."

Morgan pulled his phone out of his pocket and shook his head. "Two missed calls but I never heard the phone ring."

"Is anything wrong?" Eileen asked into the phone. "Oh dear. I'll make some of my grandmother's chicken soup. That'll make the little things feel better." She nodded once, and then again, and one last time. "Okay I'll tell him. Keep us posted and let us know if you need any help."

"Is something wrong?" Valerie asked.

Eileen shook her head. "Not really, just a bit inconvenient. Seems Fiona is running a little fever. Looks like the guys are going to get the weekend off. She doesn't want to give anyone whatever Fiona has." The woman slid her phone into her pocket and turned to Val, a very slow sly smile creeping across her face. "Looks like you boys are free to assess a ghost town."

CHAPTER FOUR

The doorbell rang and with Gray on her heels, Eileen hurried to the front door. She shouldn't have been surprised to find Valerie decked out in another magazine worthy outfit. "Good morning, welcome."

"Good morning." Slowly removing the same massive sunglasses she had on yesterday when she first rolled into the café, the woman still looked like a glamorous film star of yesteryear. Honey blonde hair was pulled back in a French twist; large button earrings in deep turquoise matched the bracelet on her wrist and the buttons on her blouse. "I don't suppose you have any coffee?"

"Absolutely. I'm not worth a damn until my second cup."

"Oh, thank heavens. I was running a little late and I barely had time for one. And that was only because Meg—who I officially declare a saint—had the good sense to hand me a travel mug as I was running out the door."

Considering Valerie wore pencil point sling back heels, even if they weren't very high, Eileen couldn't imagine her running anywhere for anything. "Please, follow this hall to the kitchen."

If Valerie had never walked the runway, Eileen would be surprised. There was an elegant air about her that was much more than city versus country. The woman knew how to strut and she wasn't even trying.

Shifting attention from her departing guest to the dog quietly seated at her feet, Eileen did a quick double take of the woman's back. Remembering the first Farraday to turn up at Abbie's after spotting Gray was Morgan, she glanced down at the dog. "Are you sure about this?"

Wise brown eyes stared up into hers, then Gray tilted his head ever so slightly, dipped his muzzle, and Eileen could almost swear she heard him answer, *Have I ever been wrong*?

On her way to the kitchen Valerie casually scanned the first floor. No sign of either cousin. She'd gone through the few outfits she'd packed and nothing seemed quite appropriate for walking a ghost town. Her favorite kitten heels were the least likely to break an ankle in. At least she'd been smart enough to leave her narrow-fitted pencil skirts home.

"The boys will be ready any moment. There was a bit of an issue with a horse getting stuck in a mud pit."

"Oh no." Even she knew mud was a dangerous thing for a horse.

Eileen laid her hand on Val's arm. "She's fine. Fortunately, Sean came across her before she could hurt herself and Morgan and Neil hurried to the east pasture to help. Needless to say, they got just a wee bit dirty getting Cinnamon free."

The sound of foot falls coming down the stairs grew closer. Not sure which brother to expect, the sight of Morgan in the doorway made her smile. Hair still damp from the fresh shower, light locks curled along his forehead, and strong muscles flexed as he turned up his shirt sleeves. But it was when the twinkling blue eyes looked up to meet hers that all the saliva in her mouth evaporated.

"Morning." He took a few steps into the room, leaned over to give his aunt a peck on the cheek, and then focused once again on her. "Neil should be ready shortly."

"Have a cup of coffee while you wait." Eileen reached for the pot.

Morgan waved his hand. "No thanks. I've drank enough coffee to energize a corpse."

"Great mind image." Val hadn't meant to spit out the first words to come to mind, but her filter seemed to still be a bit stunned by six foot of male filling the room.

"Sorry." His smile was sincere but those baby blues looked anything but apologetic.

More footfalls pounded down the steps and Val looked up. Six more feet of handsome strolled into the kitchen, but this time her mouth didn't go dry and her filter seemed to be perfectly intact. "Good morning."

"Morning." A high wattage smile took over his face and she had to admit, it was one heck of a warming grin, but even though the two brothers were clearly cut from the same mold, Neil simply didn't capture her imagination the way Morgan could. "Are we all set to go?"

"I packed a few cold drinks for y'all. The afternoon heat sneaks up on you. Added a few snacks too." Eileen tapped the top of a small cooler.

"Thanks." Morgan leaned over and gave his aunt another peck on the cheek. "I'll put this in the truck."

"I've got another cooler with some fresh pies for the church potluck. Promised the pastor I'd have them at the church by afternoon. If one of you fellows wouldn't mind putting the blue cooler on the other counter into my car that would be wonderful."

"I'll take this one." Neil lifted the larger cooler. "How many pies are in here?"

"Those are mine and Dorothy's. She brought them over this morning while y'all were wrestling the horse. No sense in both of us driving all the way to town."

"If they'll keep, I'll be happy to take them back with me after we visit Three Corners." Something about all the smiles and helping out made a person want to jump in and be helpful too. Val was no exception.

"That's very sweet of you, but I really need to get these to the church. The Ladies Church Auxiliary likes things being ready early and for church people they can get really testy if they don't have their tables set up hours before the sun sets."

Halfway to the front door, Eileen dropped like a lead balloon. Her sudden yelp had Neil setting the cooler of pies down so hard and fast that Val was a little surprised the thing didn't split open, and crossing the living room to her side in one giant launch.

Both hands clasped around her foot. "I swear I could trip over a dust bunny."

"What happened?" Morgan flew across the room faster than his brother had.

"I just tripped over my own two feet." Eileen stuck an arm up in the air. "Someone help me up?"

On one side of her Neil looped an arm around her midsection and Morgan on her other side did the same.

Eileen was barely upright when she sucked in a deep breath, squeezed her eyes shut and sighed. "Maybe this wasn't a great idea."

In a single motion, Morgan scooped his aunt into his arms and headed for the living room.

"I'll get some ice." Val turned on her heel and hurried back to the kitchen. It took a couple of tries to find the drawer with the plastic bags. Once she had it filled with ice-cubes she grabbed a dishrag, wrapped the bag in it and rushed to Eileen's side.

Standing at her shoulder, Morgan examined at his aunt's foot. "It doesn't look too bad."

Propped on the sofa by a fortress of cushions, Eileen let out a small groan. Her shoe was on the floor and her foot was already elevated high on a couple of large throw pillows. "The ice will help."

"Here you go." Gingerly, Val set the makeshift ice pack on the woman's ankle. Morgan was right, it didn't look very swollen. At least not yet. "Where do you keep the ibuprofen or aspirin?"

"Cabinet to the right of the sink. Better bring me a slice of bread to go with that."

Val nodded and was back in front of the Farraday aunt with two pills, a tall glass of milk and a biscuit. "Hope this is okay. I couldn't find any sliced bread."

"Better than okay."

Leaning forward, her hand holding the ice in place, Eileen swallowed the pills, took a few bites of the biscuit and blew out a long, slow sigh. "I don't suppose I could entreat one of you to drive those pies to church for me?"

"Of course," Morgan and Neil chorused.

Valerie even jumped in to volunteer as well. So what if she extended her visit, it wasn't like she had work waiting for her. "I can take them back to town and see Three Corners tomorrow."

"Nonsense." Eileen waved her free hand. "Surveying the ghost town is work, and work must be done."

His brow creased with concern, Morgan shook his head. "I don't know that you should be left alone."

"He has a point," Neil agreed.

Val wasn't sure which of the two looked more concerned.

"Don't be silly. This is just ranch life. It's not the first or last sprained ankle I've gotten. Just leave me the remote control and when your uncle comes in for lunch he can get me anything else I need. Besides, if I run into real trouble I can call Catherine and her or Connor will be here before I hang up the phone."

Not having any idea who Catherine and Connor were, Val could only assume they were more family and lived nearby. But like the construction cousins, she was having her doubts about taking off on a fact finding mission and leaving the family matriarch home alone.

Since no one budged, Eileen shook her head. "Really. Someone give me my phone. I'll call Catherine." She shifted in her seat and waved an arm at Neil. "Since you have the cooler, you go take the pies to town." She turned to Morgan. "And you make sure that Valerie gets to Sadieville and makes it back in one unbitten piece."

Val did not like the sound of that last statement. Until that moment she'd actually forgotten reading about Joanna's little escapade with the graveyard snakes.

"And," Eileen continued, "I'll sit here like a good little girl and wait for y'all to come back. Deal?"

Within minutes, Catherine confirmed that she would pop over shortly to check on Eileen, Neil had returned to cooler duty, and Morgan and Val were in his truck and heading down the main road on their way to the West Texas Chicken Ranch. Talk about life is what happens when you make other plans.

Even though his aunt's ankle didn't look that serious to him, Morgan still didn't like the idea of leaving her alone in that big old house.

"You're a good nephew." A slip of a smile teasing her lips, Valerie watched him much the way someone would take in the antics of a fluffy puppy. Not exactly the way he wanted most women to see him.

"I don't know about that."

"Trust me when I say that a lot of men wouldn't give a sprained ankle a second thought."

"The ankle will be fine. And I know she will too, but that doesn't mean I have to like leaving her at the house by herself."

"She won't be. You heard Catherine. She'll keep an eye out for her until one of you gets home for the rest of the day."

Morgan turned the key in the ignition and waited while the old engine roared to life. He'd had this old truck since his first construction job with his dad, and it was already used then. "I know, but it still doesn't feel right."

"And *that* is what makes you a good nephew. But honestly, your aunt doesn't strike me as the kind who would wilt away under adversity."

"Oh, trust me, a wilting flower she is not." Morgan pulled out and followed his brother's trail of dust down the long drive to the main road. She was right. Aunt Eileen wasn't like his mother. Ranch life never totally agreed with Mariah Farraday. It didn't take much to fluster her. A sprained ankle and she'd have had just about every son waiting on her hand and foot until it was completely healed and then some.

"We'll make sure not to linger. I can tell pretty fast if this is going to be the great idea I think it is or a disastrous plan."

For the duration of the ride, he was content to listen to her talk. She'd done a bit of expanding on why revitalizing an old ghost town would be appealing to investors and viewers alike. "So the idea is once it's remodeled, the buildings would be put up for sale or lease."

"Exactly. There would most likely be a mercantile or emporium. Every old west movie has a mercantile. That would be the perfect souvenir shop. Then you have the old saloon, which could most likely be turned into a restaurant. With the other town's attractions, if the food is good and the atmosphere just right, you might be amazed how many people will drive an hour or more for a special dinner."

He'd never been to Three Corners aka Sadieville himself, but even he had to admit she'd piqued his interest with her vision. Her enthusiasm was contagious. "I suppose shootouts could be staged for the tourists."

"See, now you're getting the feel for it."

"Deck the waitresses in saloon girl costume."

"Mayybee." Her response was less than enthusiastic.

His own mind was running free with ideas for a ghost town. After all, growing up, every little kid wanted to play cowboys and Indians or wild wild west. It could be a dream come true for a grown man with a lot of little kid in him. What was it his mother always said: What separates the men from the boys is the price of their toys.

CHAPTER FIVE

"Oh my." Sean Farraday took a whiff of the delicious aromas wafting through his home. "Is that chipotle rubbed ribs I smell?"

"It is." Peeling potatoes at the sink, Eileen smiled from ear to ear. "But not till dinner time."

"Tease." Hanging his hat on the nearby hook, he took a quick glance around the kitchen. Making sure they were the only ones home, he pulled his wife into his arms and kissed her soundly.

"Mmm," she mumbled, settling in against his chest. "I do like it when you do that."

"Ditto." He stole one more quick kiss and kept his arms draped about her waist until she inched back.

"Neil is in your office. He's working on some plans for a new master suite."

Sean nodded. When they married he'd given up his old master bedroom, which was little more than a slightly bigger bedroom from the others with an attached bath, and a small one at that. They'd moved into the honeymoon suite that had been done for Finn and Joanna until their house was built. Deep down they both had always known some day the space he'd once shared with Helen would need to be redone into something that was strictly his and Eileen's. Now that his nephews were available, the timing seemed as good as any. "Thought he was going out to the ghost town with Valerie and Morgan."

"Change of plans."

Sean patted her gently on the rump, held back a knowing smile, stepped back, and looked down at her feet. "I got the strangest call from Brooks."

"Oh really?" Her voice came out low and sweet and a little too coy for anyone's good.

"Something about you turning an ankle and coming into town for an x-ray."

"Mm." She pulled out a large cleaver and Sean took another step back. Dicing up peeled potatoes, she shook her head. "It was nothing."

"So you did turn your ankle?"

"Just a little twist."

"But you're fine now?"

Her knife strokes slammed a little harder against the cutting board. "Yes. Fine."

"And Neil stayed home because…" He smelled a scheme, he just didn't know what. Keeping Neil home to work on the house plans wouldn't have needed an extra layer of Eileen's intervention, or stirred up extra vigor with the knife.

"Since my ankle was sore when I first twisted it, he did me the favor of taking the pies into town for the pastor. Tonight's the singles potluck supper."

That sounded simple enough. And more than once in his life he'd turned an ankle that hurt like a sun of a gun and then later was right as rain again. But for some reason his gut told him there was more to it. And with his wife, more could be anything.

Morgan's prized pick up truck bounced down the old dirt highway. Back in its hey day the old road had been the main route from the military college to Three Corners—once upon a time known more fondly by its patrons as Sadieville.

"I suppose it could be worse." The whites on Val's knuckles told of how tightly she gripped the overhead handle. The moment the old buildings came into view her grip loosened and open mouthed, bumpy road forgotten, she leaned forward. "Oh, wow."

He'd seen the photographs of the old town and he'd

read Joanna's book on it too. Not that it came up often in conversation. Yet, the vision ahead of him was a surprise. The other unexpected find was a small Pavestone parking lot to one side of the town's entry. "The sisters must have done this."

"Someone certainly did. If it were original cobblestone I might have given the town credit but that is definitely recent construction." The second the old truck came to a stop, Valerie sprang the door handle open.

Despite the dress, and heels, and well-groomed hair, and expensive scarf carefully draped and knotted around her neck and one shoulder, all the trimmings that not only screamed city girl but very-big-city girl seemed to fade away at the childlike glee that spewed forth as she hurried up the wooden sidewalk. At the first dirty window she cupped her hands around her eyes. "This is amazing."

He had to admit, he was pretty darn impressed himself. Regardless of the age, from the splattering of brick structures to the majority of wood construction and the probability of termite infestation, the place seemed to have defied the odds and was not only still standing as Jamie had said, at least this building looked to be perfectly plumb. If he pulled out a level, he doubted it was leaning even a pinch.

"Come on!" Grinning like a kid on the way to the candy store, Valerie waved him on and trotted to the next set of windows, her grin growing even wider. "See?" She pointed up to the very faded wooden sign perched overhead. "Emporium."

To both their surprise, when she turned the knob the door opened easily.

"I guess they didn't believe in locks back in the day."

"Apparently." Her head tipped back, she followed the lines of the nine foot ceilings. "I never gave it any thought when the standard height for ceilings became only eight feet."

He'd been in construction since he was a kid helping his dad and remembered when nine footers became more popular than eight, but not once had he wondered about when the norms had changed before that. The storefront was pretty dusty, but not fifty or a hundred years worth. "I wonder if the sisters have been in here dusting too."

"I bet these barrels are as old as the town." Almost reverently, she ran her finger around the rim of the oaken wood. "Probably where they kept the salt and sugar or flour."

Watching her move from shelf to shelf, counter to counter, seeing the joy of discovery dance in her eyes, Morgan felt an inexplicable need to make sure that joy never faded. And wasn't that insane. He was a laid back hick and she was all big city sparkle.

"Oh look." She fingered a large brass ring with a few tarnished skeleton keys attached. "I guess they did have locks after all." She looked around. "Somewhere."

"Bring them along; they might open some other doors in town."

"Good idea." She slid the ring onto her wrist and took that as a cue to continue down the street. Only a few steps and her arms flew up, a single leg stepped back and a single syllable screech escaped from her lips.

"Whoa, there." Leaping forward, he caught her waistline in time to stop her from toppling over. One heel caught in the wooden walkway, if she'd fallen over she might have done some serious damage, including break that pretty little city girl neck. Easing her forward, he waited a moment to make sure she'd regained her balance. "Let's see what's going on here."

On bended knee, he gripped the heel of the shoe and tugged. Not budging an inch, that plan was not going to work. Letting his fingers wrap around her ankle, he lifted her foot from the shoe. "Might be easier to break free if you're not wearing it."

She nodded, and wobbling a moment, found her balance and slid her foot out of the shoe. "Better?"

"Better." He nodded. A few twists and tugs and the shoe was free, heel intact. "Here you go."

"Thank you." Their fingers briefly touched as he handed off the footwear, and an odd sense of loss filtered through him when she stepped out of reach.

The moment of unexpected contact gone, they passed two more storefronts, Morgan pausing just long enough to search for wood-destroying insects, deteriorating mortar, water damage, or anything else that would add to the cost of refurbishing these old buildings. Except for the first stop, he'd been quickly perusing the interiors through the dirty windows. "Good thing shiplap is popular again."

She did a three hundred and sixty degree twirl, pausing midway, just long enough to merrily shout a response. "You can thank the original Joanna Gaines for that one!"

When they reached the old brothel, Valerie stopped and took in the view, nodded her head, and then peered through the large glass doors. "Oh my."

Curious, he picked up his pace and stopped at the second of the entry doors. Oh my was definitely an understatement. The exterior of the building was painted a pristine white without a single blemish to reflect its age, but the inside was superb. Through clean glass he could see every inch of the masterful woodwork, from the closest baseboards to the staircase across the way.

Valerie inched away from the glass and her gaze lingered over the updated exterior. The flowered pots, working shutters, high gables, and restored siding. The sisters, and Jamie, had done an outstanding job.

"So." She spun around to face him. "Theoretically, the whole town could be spruced up like this."

He bobbed his chin. "Theoretically."

"I wish we could go in."

"Let's see if we can't." He pulled out his phone and texted his aunt Eileen. If the woman was resting her foot on the sofa, she'd probably be delighted to be assigned a task.

Standing close enough for him to smell the vanilla scent of her shampoo, Morgan resisted the urge to lean over and start pulling the hairpins out, one by one. Before his mind could continue down the untoward path it had embarked on, the phone dinged and he looked down.

"And there you have it." Thrilled his aunt had come through as expected, he stepped to the right of the doorway and counting three rocks from the sidewalk and two rocks back, he lifted one of the flat river rocks that were intended for decoration and retrieved the modern key.

Valerie squealed like a teenager at a pep rally and rushed up to the door. Wouldn't he just love to know if she squealed like that for other reasons.

Expectations were a tricky thing. Most of the time the sad truth of life was that few things met a person's expectations. Three Corners was most definitely not lacking. When the light bulb went off in Valerie's head, the possibilities one by one fell into place. All of it could have come crashing down if the ghost town didn't live up to her expectations. As ghost towns went, this one blew her expectations into the stratosphere.

Morgan pushed the front door open and she did another gleeful spin in place. The hem of her dress lifted slightly in the twirl and she felt like a kid again. A kid given the coveted 'it' toy. The one thing everybody wanted and only she had.

The only thing more distracting than the beautiful craftsmanship in the old bordello was the man slowly walking the room, studying the workmanship. It wasn't normal for her breath to seize at the site of a man, but this man sure had her reminding herself to inhale more than once since his booted heel struck the old wooden walkways. Even in the car, the twinkling blue eyes seemed to outshine a pool of glimmering water. Tall, handsome, polite, and brother could the men in LA learn a lesson from this guy on dumping the plastic macho attitude and being a real man, and especially how to wear an ordinary pair of jeans.

"You really don't."

Valerie blinked. Served her right for letting her mind wander off on its own. She hadn't any idea what Morgan was talking about. "Excuse me?"

His fingers slowly traveled across the carvings on the

cabinetry along the wall. "Hard to find work like this anymore."

"I feel that way every time I walk through Union Station in downtown LA and look up at the amazing ceilings." Actually, the thought crossed her mind when looking at Morgan too. "This is going to be such an easy sell."

"It is?"

"Absolutely. Who doesn't dream of going back in time, of living in a different era, having a taste of another world?"

A look of utter confusion filled Morgan's eyes. "Frankly, I can't say that I have."

"Really? Never got on a horse and considered what it would have been like to ride for days like the pioneers with nothing in the way but grass blowing in the wind and the horizon?"

"You've never ridden a horse in West Texas, have you?" he chuckled.

"I've never ridden a horse anywhere, but I assumed surely you have."

He bobbed his head. "There's a lot of nothing from Point A to Point B. We see plenty of horizon, even in Oklahoma."

"All right. Have you ever watched a war movie or film noir and wondered what it would have been like to have lived in the forties? An old western and thought those were the days?" His head tipped sideways and she knew she'd struck a nerve. "So what movie was it?"

"Abbott and Costello."

That was not what she expected.

"It was a movie about a couple of revolutionary war ghosts that were cursed to live eternity on the land where they betrayed their country. Abbott and Costello helped them prove they were patriots."

"I think I may have seen that. They lived in a tree, didn't they?"

He nodded. "I was just a kid, didn't really have a grasp on what fighting a war would really meant, but I remember wondering what would it have been like to be a part of changing history. I spent a few weeks playing Redcoats and Minuteman."

"See? Watching an old ghost town come back to life will be very appealing." She spun about to look at some of the old photos on the wall. "Wonder what the odds are that this place is haunted? A couple of friendly ghosts could be great for publicity."

Morgan choked on a laugh. "I think it's safe to say the town is ghost free."

Who needs ghosts when they have hunky hammer wielding stars? All she had to do was sell Morgan and his brothers on the idea. "There are more rooms here than I would have thought from the front."

"In order to be profitable, it would have had to have a good number of rooms for, eh, entertaining clients."

"True." Valerie felt a slight blush warm her cheeks. For a moment she'd forgotten this wasn't an ordinary boarding house or hotel. "I think I've seen enough. Time to put the numbers to work."

Waving his arm for her to lead the way downstairs, Morgan took a last look at the pristinely restored railing and banister. "It's going to be quite a project if you want to do this to the whole town."

"Not the whole town, just a few key buildings."

"The emporium?"

She nodded. "Yes, that's key. The restaurant and saloon."

"Or combine them." Morgan held the door for her then turned to lock it behind him. "Otherwise the saloon will only be open at night after the tourists go home."

The man had a point. She might have to rethink how the modern world would fit. "Which means we won't need to do the hotel if the bordello is already restored and perfectly suitable for the same purpose."

Walking beside her, Morgan hooked his hand behind his neck, then dragged it back down to his side. "The sisters did a nice job of bringing those bedrooms back to life but seems more suited to a bed and breakfast with shared baths. If you turn the saloon into a casual eatery with a nice bar, much like modern restaurants, the two places could complement each other."

They came upon the old hotel and Morgan's stepped slowed as he studied the façade. "It'll probably cost a pretty penny to properly level the old hotel, but with ensuite bathrooms it would be a true hotel." He turned the knob on the double door and turned back to Valerie. "Let's see if any of those keys work."

Val handed over the ring that was still on her wrist. Sure enough, third key in and the door unlocked. "Bingo," she squealed.

The place was empty. None of the furnishings survived. The way the cobwebs hung from every corner and fixture, it didn't look like anyone had come into this particular building.

Morgan's hand shot out behind him, his fingers stretched in invitation. "Come on. Let's take a look upstairs. But be careful, some of the steps may not be as solid as the Parlor."

Her fingers laced with his, she nodded and slowly took one step at a time. There were three floors of rooms above the main level. The hotel was the tallest building in town. "Not as big as I'd thought."

"Not small either." He opened the door to one bedroom, then another. "There's an even number of rooms which should make it easy to turn each one into a nice bath and closet and add a foot or so to the sleeping rooms."

"I like how this is looking."

"Good bones. That's all you need." At the end of the hall, the top floor had an extra door. Morgan slowly turned the knob and exposed another staircase. "Must lead to the roof."

"Shall we take a look?"

"Might as well."

At the top of the stairs, another door opened to a flat top roof the expanse of the building.

"Oh wow." From pretty much anywhere between Tuckers Bluff and Three Corner's a person could see for miles and miles, but from up here the same view looked totally different. Spectacular.

"One more thing to add to the appeal of a luxury hotel. There's enough space on the ground floor that you could add a restaurant."

"I thought we were turning the Saloon into a restaurant?"

"Yes, but hear me out. I've heard my cousins mention more than once that there aren't enough places to go out for a nice dinner without driving to Butler Springs. That means if done right, this place could hold a lot of commercial possibilities. I mean, besides your new show."

He was right, of course. Turning her back on the breathtaking view, she followed him down the stairs. Val needed to think outside her usual box. At first the only thing she cared about were the potential ratings from restoring an old ghost town in front of the camera. Rehab TV, even an entire town, was something she understood. Creating something marketable in the end that was painfully close to an adult amusement park was a little jarring and out of her league.

Silently, they descended to the lobby and took one last look before leaving.

Morgan locked the door and handed her back the keys. "If you think about it, if you could talk a chef into taking a chance on it, you might even be able to make this into a five star restaurant."

"Okay." Val stopped in her tracks. "You dream even bigger than me. No one loves fine dining as much as me. Any table setting with more than one spoon, fork and knife will make me drool. When a waiter knows to serve from the left and remove plates from the right I get downright giddy. But I don't see Thomas Keller opening a restaurant out here."

Morgan chuckled. He should have known she wasn't one to eat but rather to dine. More than just her wardrobe separated this city girl from his reality. And she was right, fine dining was as likely to be a staple in this part of the country as a snow mobile in summer. "Maybe five stars is overreaching a bit, but a really good restaurant could conceivably attract more than just tourists. As much as I love the pub and Frank's cooking at the café, my cousins are right. Assuming I wanted to take a girl on a date and pull out all the stops, there just isn't anywhere near to go. There are plenty of residents around Tuckers Bluff who would drive a good spell to celebrate an anniversary, engagement, or birthday someplace special."

Special. Looking over her shoulder, she scanned the buildings along the street. Many of them would have to be repurposed. She'd been thinking shops for crafts, or books, but what if… "A spa."

"Excuse me?"

"A truly luxury hotel with fine dining and a spa and all the things that make an out of the way spot a destination. So much could be done with that spectacular rooftop view."

"Now you're getting the idea."

"If I can sell the idea and bring in the investors." She nodded to herself. "Yep, this will make for one beauty of a television show."

"Still thinking about reality TV?"

"Of course."

"Then you'd better have some darn good project managers on hand. Building a city isn't easy."

She was well aware she'd need better than good to juggle the construction schedule, the productions schedule, and the media that was no doubt going to show up from time to time.

"You're frowning." He wiped a finger across her brow. "Change your mind?"

She shook her head.

"Because that would be the sensible thing to do."

"Perhaps. But no one ever said I was sensible. What I was thinking is that I'm going to have to spend more time here in Texas than in LA."

"I'm not sure if you're crazy or brilliant." They reached the truck and he opened the door for her, tossed that dazzling smile that could probably win over the Wicked Witch of the West, then closed the door to circle the hood and climb in on the driver side.

Buckled into his seat, she waited till he'd turned the key and started the engine. "What would you say if told you I want you and your brothers to be a part of this?"

One hand on the steering wheel, his head whipped back from looking out the rear window and somewhere between shock and amusement, he let out a soft chuckle. "Now I know the answer. You're crazy."

CHAPTER SIX

Beyond the shadow of any doubt, Valerie was delusional. His world, his brothers' lives were in Oklahoma. A project the magnitude of what she was talking about would take months, or longer. The logistics would be a nightmare. Then there was the issue of television cameras. Definitely not the type of crew he would want on his construction site.

"I'm not crazy." She pulled on her seatbelt shoulder strap and shifted slightly to better see him. "I'm very good at what I do and I'm positive this will be a hit."

"That part I believe. You've convinced me that deep down everyone has a memory tucked away of wanting to be transported back, or forward, in time."

"Forward?"

"Star Trek has been reinvented over and over."

She shrugged a shoulder and rolled her eyes slightly. "Well, if you want to look at it that way, even in the futuristic shows, someone always wants to return to the allure of the Wild West. And this place definitely has that."

Has that Wild West allure certainly hit the nail on the head. A few times he could almost see the long-skirted women wearing colorful bonnets or twirling parasols, making their way down the wooden walkway. He could already picture an afternoon showdown. Every day at two o'clock, the cowboys burst out of the old saloon and stare each other down from opposite ends of the main road to the delight of all the tourists. Yes, she got that one right. Even the *Brady Bunch* at one point found a way to strand the family in the treasured ghost town concept.

"You're thinking about it, aren't you?" Valerie

interrupted his thoughts.

"The town? Yes. But not being the ones to wield a hammer."

The rear truck bed bounced over a rut in the road and he wondered if whoever climbed onboard for this deal was going to pave the darn thing or leave it as part of the old west ambiance.

"You're still thinking about it." She grinned, leaning back against the car door.

What was she, a mind reader? How could she possibly know what was going on his head? There was no way he wanted any part of it. Though some of the craftsmanship surprised him, drew him in. He'd always thought old west or mining towns were tossed together on the fly. The old theater was one of the few buildings boarded up. Made him wonder what was inside. Would there be more ornate woodwork. Would everything be perfectly plumb and level? How hard would it be to bring the old place into the twenty-first century? Could it even be done without breaking the bank? And how much would that bank be? Would the network or whoever is footing the bill want it done right or done fast? After all, isn't television all about the illusion? On the other hand, how else would they get a return on their investment if they didn't hand over a quality product to an end user who knows how to turn this old ghost town into a profitable empire?

So deep in his own thoughts, he hadn't noticed Val loosen her seatbelt more and twist further around so she was almost completely facing him.

"You want to do it, don't you?" Her eyes glimmered with satisfaction.

"Not so fast. Yes, the project is unique. But our getting involved? No." Except he had to admit the more he mulled over the possibilities, the more intrigued he was by the whole idea. Of all the jobs his family's business had taken on through the years, the true restoration projects had always been his favorite, and something told him Neil would be all over the designs for this place like white on rice. But a project of this size would keep most of his brothers away from Oklahoma for months. His mother would have a cow if she couldn't keep an eye on most of her chicks for that long. And that didn't even begin to cover the fit she'd throw if she knew it was in what she'd deemed forbidden Texas Farraday country. Not to mention juggling their crews. "Besides, why us? Why not some of your regular teams from your other shows?"

"Oh." She sat back straight.

"You don't even know what kind of workmanship we do. We could be the worst contractors this side of the Mississippi."

"I doubt that." Her impish grin returned.

"For what it's worth, we're not, but that doesn't change the question. Why not use crews you've worked with before?"

"Well, for starters," she twisted around to face him again, "all of those crews are in LA or Vancouver, not Texas."

He would give her that one. Just thinking about moving crews from Oklahoma was a logistics nightmare; dealing with California or Canada could only make it worse. "And?"

Valerie leaned forward. "What do you mean 'and'?"

"You said for starters. Where's the rest?"

"Oh." She flopped back in her seat. "Nothing much."

"I doubt that. You're very deliberate in your wording. I don't see any reason why this would be any different."

"Well, if you must know," her hands clasped in her lap, "looks are important on television. A little baby fat puts even more pounds on in the camera's eye."

He nodded slowly. This wasn't the first time he'd heard about the camera adding poundage to a person. Apparently there was some truth to it.

"And my teams aren't related."

"What's that have to do with anything?"

"Haven't you ever watched the home remodeling shows?"

"A few." Not in their entirety. He watched an episode or two with his mother, but nothing he could specifically remember.

"Well, the most popular ones are usually married couples—"

"That should let us off the hook," he cut her off, "we're all single."

"Or brothers."

It *was* a family business.

"In this case they want a new twist, so construction cousins would fit the bill." Her arms folded across her chest. "And not a fat, ugly one in the bunch."

He couldn't help the chuckle that erupted. "Nice of you to say so, but you haven't met all my brothers."

Immediately, her hands dropped to her sides, brows tented high on her forehead, her jaw dropped, her mouth hung slightly open, and her eyes rounded in what could only be described as utter shock. "You have ugly brothers?"

This time Morgan laughed outright. "I didn't say that."

Valerie huffed the way his mom did whenever one of her sons got the better of her in a family squabble.

"Besides, we're not cousins. As you said, we're brothers."

"Technicality. Home base is Texas so you'd be pitched as the Oklahoma cousins, even though the ones doing the construction would be brothers. Then there'd be a few cameos from the Texas Farradays. Showing off the work, that sort of thing. Not all reality TV is strictly OTF."

"OTF?"

"On the fly. Some, actually most, is very much scripted and planned. So the idea really is perfect." That look in her eyes of sheer satisfaction was back.

And they were back to square one in the battle of wills. Already he could see the arch ahead for the entry to Connor's place and his uncle's only a short distance beyond that. He hadn't realized they'd been on the road that long. A part of him wished he could miss the turn and keep going, continue battling it out just the two of them. After all, wasn't the best part of a disagreement the making up?

There wasn't a doubt in her mind that Morgan Farraday was more than interested in her plan. Well, maybe not the TV stardom portion of it, but definitely resuscitating that old town. She could see it in the twinkle of his eyes every time he looked at what was and pictured in his mind what could be. A man like him didn't work to earn a paycheck, men like the Farradays were motivated by something deeper, stronger. If it wasn't family, or community, maybe it was art or history, something. She wasn't sure which it was for Morgan, but as sure as she was standing in the middle of West Texas, that man wanted a part of it. She could feel it in her bones, if she could just get him to stop fighting it.

"We're here." He hopped out of his truck and muttered a muffled curse.

It took her a few seconds to compute what he'd actually said. The reaction was so unlike the behavior she'd observed from any of the Farradays since her arrival.

Next he kicked the door shut with his foot and holding his hands in front of him, lips tightly pressed together, he circled the hood and used both hands to open her door. "Sorry about that. I've been meaning to get that trim fixed."

"I've heard worse." Way worse. The odd way he held his hands had her glancing over. The moment she spotted the trickle of blood easing between his finger-tight grip on his other hand, she realized why he'd cursed. "You cut yourself."

He shrugged. "Not the first time."

The steady thin flow of red told her it was a bigger deal than he was letting on. Without any thought, she pulled her new Egyptian cotton scarf away from her neck and grabbed his hand. A quick glance and she hurriedly wrapped her scarf around his hand, tugging back at it when he tried to pull it away.

"That's a nice scarf. I'll wash it off inside."

"You need pressure." She gripped the hand. "Wouldn't be surprised if you need stitches."

He stopped trying to pull his hand back. "It's nothing."

"Hold it up." Gripping his wrist, she lifted his hand. "Needs to be higher than your heart to slow the bleeding.

Let's get you inside, clean it up and then see if you need stitches."

One side of his face lifted in a lazy smile and he dipped his chin. "Yes, ma'am, but it's really not that bad."

"Men. If I pull my hand away, can you apply pressure and keep your hand where it is until we get inside?"

Twinkling eyes smiled at her. "I think so."

"And stop making fun of me. This is serious."

To stop from smiling, he bit down on his lower lip, but the laughter in his eyes gave away his amusement with the situation.

"Men," she muttered again. "Never mind. I'll hold it. Let's go." Leaving her purse in the car, she squeezed his bleeding hand between hers and stomped to the front door.

"I wasn't making fun of you. I just find the idea of my hand bandaged in a scarf that probably costs more than my boots…entertaining. I really can do this."

"What you can do is open the door with your good hand. Please."

"Yes, ma'am." Morgan nodded, turned the knob and shoved the door open.

The entry opened to the large and empty living room to the right. Valerie had expected to find his aunt still resting on the sofa. "Let's get to the kitchen."

"Good idea. Smells delicious."

Even though he couldn't see her face, she still rolled her eyes at him.

"I wonder if Aunt Eileen is in her room." Morgan shifted right, changing their trajectory.

Valerie gave his arm a light tug. "Oh no you don't. You can check on Eileen in a minute. First, let's see how you're doing." Opening a nearby drawer, she pulled out a couple of dishrags, hoping the ones she'd chosen didn't turn out to be any of Eileen's favorites. "I don't suppose you know where the bandages and antiseptics are kept?"

He shook his head. "Sorry."

If his hand was as bad as she thought, she might have to go through the house in search of what she needed or someone who knew where it might be. On a whim, she opened the doors on the two nearest upper cabinets, surprised to find one filled with almost everything she needed. Mostly filled with bottled medicine and over the counter cough remedies, she did find some antibacterial cream and a box of assorted Band-aids.

First aid items and dishrags ready on the counter, she glanced up at her patient in time to catch Morgan following her actions with unexpected tenderness in his gaze. Blinking hard, she returned to the task at hand, slowing when she felt his arm tense. "Does that hurt?"

He shook his head. "Not really."

"Not really?" She shook her head again and continued unwrapping. Morgan had been right about one thing—she'd spent way too much money on the boutique scarf. On the other hand, the cotton fabric was proving to be an excellent bandage. The wound fully exposed wasn't nearly as large a gash as she'd thought at first glimpse.

"Told you it was nothing."

"Maybe." Wetting down one of the rags, she cleaned away the drying blood. Already the skin seemed to be closing up, only to have a trickle of blood reappear at the lack of pressure. Quickly she opened the seal on a large non-stick bandage pad, squirted a bit of the cream on it and placed it just tight enough over the injury. "It doesn't look bad enough for stitches, but I don't suggest you do any arm wrestling tonight."

Morgan bobbed his head. "No problem."

"I would like to tape it for extra pressure." She gently pressed his treated wound up toward his shoulder, the easiest way to keep it above his heart and keep him for over-using it.

"Thank you," he lowered his hand, "but it's okay."

Once again, she gently pushed it back to his shoulder. "It can be okay up here."

The back door swung open and slammed shut.

"You're back." Sean Farraday hung his hat on a nearby hook. "How'd it go?"

"Great." Val smiled and pointed a thumb at Morgan. "Only a minor casualty."

Steel blue eyes narrowed under thick dark brows, carefully studying the scene before him. "What happened?"

"Nothing really." Morgan lifted his hand away from his chest to show his uncle. "Caught the loose trim on the car door just right and got a little cut."

"That artwork on the counter got anything to do with the little cut?" His nose twitched in the direction of the blood-stained yellow scarf.

Even Valerie had to agree that the damage looked much worse than it was if the only thing to go by was the soiled scarf. "He should be fine if doesn't overdo it."

"Oh, his aunt will make sure of that."

"Speaking of which," Morgan glanced toward the living room, "how's the ankle doing?"

"Fine."

"I expected to find her parked on the couch for the next few days."

Sean shook his head. "More like parked in the barn. We've got another rejected calf. All hands are on deck keeping those two fed and loved on."

"Oh, how sad." Valerie could only assume the mama cows had done the rejecting.

The back door blew open and Aunt Eileen stomped her feet hard on the rear mat.

"Ankle looks pretty good," Morgan teased.

His aunt's face momentarily blanched before she plastered on a bright smile and nodded. "Yes, I am very fortunate. Could have been so much worse."

Val wasn't sure but she could have sworn she noticed uncle and nephew exchange a curious glance. What they were saying to each other, she didn't know.

"Well," Morgan stepped forward, looped an arm around his aunt, and kissed the top of her head, "I'm glad you're okay."

"Wish I could say the same about you. Why are you holding your hand like you've got a mean case of heartburn?"

"The car bit him." Head in the fridge, Sean pulled out a bottle of milk.

Valerie had no idea milk still came in bottles, anywhere.

At Eileen's wide-eyed stare, Morgan chuckled. "Cut my hand. I'm fine now."

Eyes still rounded, Eileen reached for his hand, turned it left than right. Frowning, she lifted her gaze to meet his. "You tend to this?"

Morgan's head turned back and forth. "We have Florence Nightingale over here to thank."

"Hardy har har." Valerie resisted the urge to stick her tongue out at him like a little kid and instead faced his aunt.

Eileen's gaze shifted from Morgan's hand to Valerie, then caught sight of the scarf before returning to Morgan. "Strikes me you owe the girl a new scarf."

"Yes, ma'am. I do." He tipped his chin toward the back door. "How's the horse doing?"

"Good. You should take her a carrot." At the sink, his aunt washed her hands. "Got a bunch in the pantry."

He nodded.

"Bring Valerie. Show her the barn."

Barn? Valerie wasn't all too sure about that. Didn't they smell? Like, well, smell.

"Follow me. I'll introduce you to Cinnamon."

The path to the barn was well lit and easier to walk than she'd expected. Once inside, she was delighted to note that it didn't smell anything like she'd expected.

"You're frowning." He closed the door behind her.

"Sorry. I was expecting it to smell…"

"Stinky?" He smiled.

"Yeah."

"Stalls are mucked often. Mostly the air is filled with the scent of hay and leather. And occasionally manure, but mostly hay and leather. Especially after a hard rain."

A few feet in, he paused at a Dutch door and turned the latch. "How's it going, girl?"

Valerie had to admit, she wouldn't mind having the man coo at her in that low rolling tone. She took a step forward and then froze in place.

"It's all right. She won't hurt you."

"She's huge."

"Only sixteen hands."

"Hands?" she managed to mutter, still rooted firmly in place. She didn't want to check but was willing to bet a year's salary the horse's teeth were huge as well. And painful.

"Usually about four inches. Size is determined by measuring from floor to the highest point of the horse's withers."

There was no point in asking what withers were. She might as well quit while she was still at a safe distance.

He scratched the horse's ear. The animal wiggled her lips, rolled her head and Val took a step back. "If you rub right down her nose, she'll be your friend for life."

"Thanks, but I'll pass." What she really wanted was to turn and run.

"I'm gathering that means you don't want to give her a carrot?" Pulling one from his pocket, he laid it on his flat open palm.

Valerie's suspicions about the horse's teeth were confirmed. She shook her head and asked herself for the first time in days, what in the heck was a city girl like her doing in a place like this?

CHAPTER SEVEN

"Mom will bust a gut." Large platter of cornbread in hand, Morgan passed it to his right. "You haven't told her we're helping Adam this trip either, have you?"

Neil shook his head.

"See?" Morgan waved an arm at this brother. "How could we possibly explain being here for months on a project of that size?"

"We could work in shifts." Neil passed the bread platter to his aunt. "As long as one of us was home for a few weeks at a time, Mom probably won't notice that this isn't any old project in some random Texas location."

"What I don't understand," Joanna lifted a rib from her plate, "is why would having y'all here specifically be a problem for your mother?"

That same question had crossed his mind more than once since coming to town when they helped rebuild Chloe's house. His gaze locked with his brother's. Neil didn't look to have a better answer to the question than he did. None of the brothers did.

"It's complicated." His uncle Sean forked a spare rib onto his dish.

Finn shrugged. "I always liked Aunt Mariah. She used to bring Grace and me candy whenever she and Uncle Pat visited. I loved those Pixie Sticks."

"Straight sugar," Uncle Sean groused.

Hannah held her hands up. "Okay, let's assume you can get around your mother's objections. Do you even want to get involved with the ghost town?"

"I would like to at least have a look for myself," Neil

answered before Morgan could respond.

"First of all," Morgan waved a fork at his brother, "we don't know anything about television production. Having cameras and crews around us could be a nightmare. Besides, don't they say these shows are all staged?"

Neil shrugged. "No clue."

Lips pressed tightly, Aunt Eileen tipped her head to one side and hefted a shoulder. "They do say that about a lot of the most popular shows."

"There you go." Morgan turned back to his brother. "Who has time to refurbish *and* act? Then, despite Valerie's enthusiasm over this project, neither of us knows how serious she is about having us involved."

"Why wouldn't she be serious?" Joanna asked. "After all, you certainly fit the bill."

"What?" Morgan and Neil echoed.

The three women at the table rolled their eyes.

"You're exactly what any producer would want." Aunt Eileen blew out a long breath. "There are multiple places that the tall, dark, and handsome nature of the Farraday mold would be in high demand."

Sean coughed and cleared his throat.

"Besides there." Aunt Eileen glared at her husband, and Joanna actually blushed. Holding up two fingers, Eileen pointed to one. "Romance novel cover," then the other finger, "and Reality TV stars would be top of the list."

Morgan had learned a long time ago that the Farraday genetics could often open doors for them, but when it came to the important things in life, a pretty face wasn't worth the price of a postage stamp. It hadn't helped a bit when Carolyn turned him down from bended knee to his empty bank account and finally understanding that the family money wasn't his to spend as she willed. He swallowed the bad taste the memory left in his mouth and looked to his aunt. "Actually, Valerie mentioned our being related. The Oklahoma cousins to the Texas based clan. But mostly I think she likes the alliteration in the title."

"There's that too." Eileen held up another finger. "I wonder if she'll be back often to check out the production?"

"I'm pretty sure she's only on the acquisitions side of things." Joanna licked some sauce from her thumb. "She'd only be involved in the negotiations, not the implementations. At least, I think that's what she said when she optioned the rights to my other book."

"Nope." Morgan eased his head left then right. "She specifically told me she'd be around to see it through."

Joanna shrugged. "I may have misunderstood. There was a lot going on that day. Besides, optioning my book is very different. Lots of books get optioned and are never sold into production, but for the rehab idea she already has a taker."

"So she'd be sticking around." Neil smiled at Joanna's comment. "That could be interesting."

Morgan didn't like the gleam in his brother's eye any better than he had when Neil had met Valerie at the café.

"I wonder if she owns a pair of jeans." Aunt Eileen's face pinched in thought.

"Good point." Sean nodded. "Not a single woman I know from these parts would be running about that broken down town in a dress and high heels. Or much of anywhere around here for that matter."

"At least," Hannah piped in, "they weren't very high heels."

Sean shook his head. "High or low, a heel sinks just the same in dry sand."

"I'm sure she owns sensible shoes and more clothing than the expensive accessories we've seen so far." Aunt Eileen waved a hand at her husband. "Who can blame her for wanting to be a part of reviving Sadieville?"

Thinking back on how excited Valerie had gotten with every new discovery made Morgan smile. Actually, just about everything with her today made him want to smile, even her braving the dust covered town in high heels and a dress.

"And what has you grinning like a cat with a bowl of cream?" His aunt looked down her nose at him.

"Just thinking about walking the old town."

"Uh-huh." His aunt kept her gaze fixed on him.

"It was almost fun watching the town come to life

through her eyes. You should have seen how she nearly salivated over the idea of a hotel resort with fine dining and a spa."

"Fine dining?" Fork frozen midway to his mouth, Sean's gaze bookended his wife's. "Hope she doesn't expect to find any of that in Tucker's Bluff."

"I'm sure she doesn't." There was no point in debating her expectations. After only a few hours with Valerie, Morgan had no doubt her expectations for lowly West Texas were anything but high. She was a big city girl through and through. Although, his gaze dropped to his bandaged hand, without hesitation she'd taken charge and not flinched at the sight of blood, nor given a second thought to using her fashionable scarf. For sure, at least this big city girl was no wuss.

The tea kettle whistled and Meg turned off the burner. "How did it go?"

"Better than I expected." The entire drive back to town from the ranch, Valerie had been processing all the thoughts bouncing around in her head. She'd been sorely tempted to accept Eileen's invitation to stay for dinner, if for no other reason than her braised ribs smelled divine. But so many ideas had been kicked about on her visit to the old town that she needed time for everything to gel. Besides, if she were honest with herself, sitting at the same table with Morgan Farraday would have been too much of a distraction. Something about that man was seriously hard to resist. Maybe it was the hat. Or the boots.

Who was she kidding? The slightest of smiles sent her stomach doing somersaults, and the twinkle in his eyes when he looked at her made her heart dance. She was acting like a hormonal teen. She really needed to get a grip and concentrate on work. She had business to figure out.

"Knock knock." A woman's voice carried down the hall.

"In the kitchen, Becky," Meg called out.

"Hi." A pretty brunette with a ponytail dangling down her back bounced into the room. "Caitlin went right to sleep and DJ is glued to the sports channel. So of course I came here."

"Just in time too." Meg opened the oven door. "Blueberry crumb cake is ready."

"You're *baking*?" The utter surprise in the woman's voice led Val to believe this was something out of the ordinary.

"Of course not." Meg set the warm pan on a cooling rack. "Toni made it. All I did was slide it into the oven and wait for the timer to ding."

The brunette flopped onto a nearby stool. "Oh thank goodness. I don't know that I could've turned down blueberry crumb cake even if you had baked it."

Meg rolled her eyes. "I'm not that bad. Becky, say hello to Valerie Moore. Becky is my sister-in-law. She's married to DJ, my husband's brother."

Not even another minute passed by when Abbie from the café trotted in, making the rounds hugging everyone. "My feet are killing me. I'm ready to sink into a sea of down feathers."

"Then you don't want a slice of crumb cake?" Meg teased.

"Of course I do. I may be tired but I'm not stupid." Just to assure everyone, she leaned up a little straighter, eyeing the cooling cake. "I swear the world has gone nuts. Felix brought this week's copy of the paper in. All anyone could talk about was the piece on the dogs. Seems there's a black market for stolen pedigree dogs. Ever since some character got a six-figure reward for returning a movie star's dog, it's become big business."

"I read that they suspect the person who stole the dog and collected the reward are probably the same and," Meg pointed at Abbie, "a French bulldog was stolen right out of the mayor of Butler Springs' yard. They found him when the new owner who paid almost ten grand for it, took it to the vet for a check up and they found the chip."

Becky shook her head. "So glad we don't have to deal with crazy stuff like that here in Tuckers Bluff."

"I'm back." The woman introduced to Val earlier as another sister-in-law, Toni, bounced into the room, leaned over to give Becky a kiss on the cheek and landed in the seat beside Valerie. "Helen has really become a model child at bedtime. Brooks isn't on call tonight so I decided I wouldn't mind a little of that crumb cake I left you."

"Then you're here just in the nick of time." Becky laughed.

Valerie didn't know what was in the water, but these women had hugging hello down to a science and were all full of pep and energy. "Is it always this busy at night?" She hoped that didn't come off to the others as snarky as it sounded to her own ears.

Pulling a stack of plates from the cupboard, Meg shook her head. "Not usually, but sometimes when the stars align we'll get the chance to hang out together." She sent out a dish in front of each woman, and one more.

"Are we expecting someone else?"

All the women nodded.

Meg slid a slice of cake onto her dish. "Odds are pretty good that if Allison drives by and sees all the cars out front, she's going to stop too. The woman works too hard."

"Another sister-in-law?"

"Ethan's wife. She and Brooks run the new hospital here in town."

"Besides," Toni handed out forks, "she's gonna want to hear firsthand all about Hollywood coming to Tuckers Bluff."

"Wait a minute." Becky held up her hands. "Since when is Hollywood coming to Tuckers Bluff?"

Toni reached for a napkin. "Since Valerie here decided to do a reality TV show with the Oklahoma cousins fixing up the old ghost town."

"Should be a big hit." Meg set her glass down. "There are plenty of women, fans of decorating shows or not, who would tune in to watch any Farraday brother for thirty minutes a week, regardless of whether or not they have a clue how to hammer a nail."

"Add to that the fun of watching something so filled with history come back to life, that's seriously cool." So engrossed with their cake and companionship, none of the women noticed the brunette, most likely the doctor they were expecting, who had quietly entered the room and picked up on the conversation without skipping a beat. "I especially love the idea of the spa."

Val wasn't so sure how these people knew so much about her show when she'd barely put the pieces together herself this afternoon.

Toni put her fork down. "I admit I'm especially intrigued by who will be tagged to run the nice restaurant. This town really does need something a little fancier than the café or the pub." The pretty blonde leaned over and patted Abbie's knee. "No offense intended."

Abbie shook her head and waved an arm at her sister-in-law. "None taken. I get tired of Frank's cooking sometimes too."

"I freely admit DJ's a better cook than I am," Becky bragged on her husband. "I'm guessing it's because Aunt Eileen is better than my grandmother. And heaven knows my mother couldn't boil water."

"Well, I cook just fine." Toni rubbed her curled fingertips against her shoulder.

"You don't count." Meg waved a finger at her longtime friend. "You're Italian. Cooking delicious food is part of your DNA."

"Still," Toni turned to Valerie, "it's nice to have something put in front of you that was cooked with ingredients you'll never find in your own refrigerator."

"Good to know." Val smiled at Toni. "But how do you guys know so much about this? I've been back for less than an hour."

Meg was the first to chuckle. "I suspect Aunt Eileen mentioned it to one of the afternoon social club ladies."

"From there," Toni looked to Valerie, "they most likely spread it to half the town."

"And that half," Abbie reached for her teacup, "came to

the café to share with the rest of town."

"I see." Not that she had any secrets—yet—but she was going to have to remember the Tuckers Bluff communication network was more efficient than Western Union.

"So," Becky reached for another piece of cake, "I hear this could take months. Will you be here that long?"

"I don't know yet." Val didn't even have a green light from anyone, but she knew with the networks wanting her to do another rehab series, this concept was a slam dunk.

"I understand Neil wants to go look." Meg sliced more cake.

"Really?" That was good news. "I wonder if he has time tomorrow?"

The women looked left to right in an oddly coordinated silent message. Valerie's life didn't exactly include hanging out with a lot of women friends. Actually, other than Marilyn, her career path hadn't left her a lot of time for friends since college. LA was spread far and wide and careers and lifestyle changes made hanging out with friends in her business tough. Still, she got the feeling she was the only person in the room not in on some secret. "Am I missing something?"

Meg sucked in a long breath. "Do you own any, ehm, sensible shoes?"

"Of course I do." That was a silly question. "Gucci makes some great wedges for when I have to do a lot of walking."

That same look passed from one in-law to another.

Meg bobbed her chin once. "I was thinking of something more rugged. Like cowboy boots or something with laces."

Laces?

Becky swallowed her last bite and grinned up at her. "What about jeans? You have to have jeans."

Slowly, she nodded. Though she had a feeling the $200 denims hanging in her closet at home weren't what these women had in mind.

"You don't look terribly convinced," Allison said

through a thin smile. "As a former Northern Cali girl, I'm going to guess the jeans you're thinking of aren't anything you'd want to wear around concrete or paint?"

Val felt her eyes round as though she'd stuck her wet finger in a high volt socket.

"Thought so." Allison walked to the tea kettle. "You look to be Meg's size."

"I have a couple of pairs I haven't fit in since Fiona was born. You can have your pick."

"If you wear size eight shoes, I have a pair of snazzy boots that are a little big for me," Toni piped in. "You can have them."

"Boots?" she muttered.

"Have you ever tried a pair on?" Toni hopped off her seat, empty cup in hand. "Once they're broken in those suckers are more comfortable than my bedroom slippers."

"No one," Meg shook her head, "wants to give up a well broken-in pair of boots. Neither man nor woman."

By the time the hen party was over, she'd consumed more crumb cake than she had all year, she had not one but two pairs of the softest fitting jeans she'd ever worn, Toni had run home and back to deliver one butter soft pair of cowboy boots that might as well have been custom made for her, and Becky donated a real cowboy—or would that be cowgirl—hat that would definitely keep the shade off her face. Standing in front of the mirror, even with her own neatly pressed button down shirt, she looked like she'd fallen off the cover of Southwest Ranch and Family. The look wasn't her at all, but holy moly if she didn't rock it.

CHAPTER EIGHT

"How's the hand doing?"

After only a couple of days—and a few hours at that—of hearing that voice, he knew it instantly. The odd thing was how the mere sound of it made him want to smile. Setting the tray of drywall compound on the ground, he turned to see Valerie standing in the doorway. Blinking twice, he almost raised his hands to swipe the disbelief from his eyes. The last thing he'd expected to see was a woman who, except for the colorful scarf tied loosely around her neck and those huge dark glasses perched on her head, looked as though she were born and raised in West Texas. While his brain thought *wow*, his mouth muttered, "Nice boots."

She lifted her toes, rolling back on her heels. "The girls were right. They're pretty comfortable."

"They look good on you." Everything looked good on her. Too good.

"Thanks." She tipped her chin in the direction of his hands. "I guess it's doing all right?"

He bobbed his head and wiggled his fingers. "Every once in a while it reminds me that it's been cut, but for the most part it's in just the right spot not to interfere too much with holding tools."

"Good. I know how much getting all this finished means to Meg and yesterday was pretty much shot thanks to our trip out to Three Corners."

"With Neil helping we've got the new sheetrock up and taped and bedded. We'll blow some texture on next and while it dries we can run Neil out to the town."

She turned her head, scanning the room. "Where is he?"

"We're running a little low on the drywall compound so he's picking up an extra bag while I finish this up."

"Well, I guess I'd better let you finish." She took a step back and did a half turn, giving him another glimpse of how well the jeans hugged her figure.

"I'm actually done." And a good thing too. He'd been able to tuck the original version of Valerie – like he had Carolyn – into the same box labeled ambitious city girls. This new rendition was just a pinch too distracting. "Just have to rinse off these tools and then I'm all yours." Her eyes widened for just an instant before a smile crossed her face, and he quickly wished he'd picked another phrase. "Sorry, I didn't mean…"

"Too bad." She spun on her boot heel and, for a California girl, did a great job of sashaying out the door. Maybe it was the boots, but somehow he didn't think so.

Everything set aside and wiping his hands, the door to the private apartment opened and for a moment Morgan thought it might be Valerie again.

"Well, that was an interesting walk through town." Neil dropped the bag and a few other items on the floor by the door. "Seems the sisters are all riled up."

"Riled? Those sweet old ladies?"

Neil rolled his eyes at his brother. "I'm not kidding. They, like everyone else in town, heard that Valerie wants to do a reality TV show set in Three Corners."

"And they don't like the idea of someone else vying for their ancestor's town?"

Neil shook his head. "Not at all. It seems they've wanted collaborators to step up and do things to improve the town, but they gave up because of the ghosts."

Morgan coughed on his own spit. "Excuse me?"

"You heard me. They think the place is haunted."

The urge to laugh was overwhelming, but the serious expression painted on his brother's face didn't look to be a laughing matter. "You're not kidding, are you?"

"Not even a little bit. Even though you and I know better than to believe in ghosts, those two sisters are convinced that some woman is haunting the place. It may sound crazy to us but to them it's very real. Apparently, that's the reason they stopped fixing the town up themselves."

"Well, that's ridiculous. We all know old houses creek in the dark of night, wind blows through chimneys and cracks, all you need is a few squawking owls in the mix and you can scare just about any mortal with a vivid imagination."

"All I know is they were pretty convinced and seemed almost apoplectic at the idea that we're considering more than a single daylight visit."

"So the ghost or ghosts only comes out at night?"

Neil shrugged. "They weren't terribly specific. Believe it or not, I was trying my best to escape so we can get out there and back in time to have this room painted for Meg before nightfall."

"And that's the key word. No matter who takes on the project, if anyone does at all, I doubt they'll be doing much night work."

"Well, if we don't get boogying, we'll be the ones doing night work." Neil reached for the door knob. "Who's driving, big brother?"

"You know I am. No one drives my truck but me."

"Wasn't sure if you and your truck were squabbling after she bit you." Neil held back a laugh. "You know how fickle women can be."

One step behind his brother on the stairs, Morgan lightly whacked the back of his kid brother's head. "I'm still doing the driving."

The three of them had hardly stepped out the front door when Neil's phone rang. "Farraday."

Morgan's hand gently rested on Val's back, nudging her down the steps. The simple gesture made her feel oddly special, and safe.

"Yes, Mr. Harrigan. Give me one second, please." Neil

tapped at his phone. "It's Harrigan on that Tulsa job we bid on. Give me ten minutes."

Morgan nodded. "From what little I know about Harrigan, those ten minutes will be at least twenty, maybe more."

"We can go back inside and wait?"

"Actually, I think I want to take a short stroll over to Sisters. Have a little talk."

"About the ghosts?"

"You've heard about that?"

"Oh, yeah." When she'd stopped by after breakfast to kick around their part as the sole owners of any specific property in town with her ideas, the sisters had given her an earful and half. "It seems they were spooked."

"I heard."

Again, his hand rested on her lower back, directing her down the street and she wished there was an excuse for him to leave it there.

"Old houses creek, whistle, and rattle. The peace and quiet of the dead of night makes them sound even louder."

"Do old houses also scream for help?"

Morgan stopped dead in his tracks. "What?"

"A woman's voice crying "help me" over and over. That's what sent the two sisters running, and they haven't gone back."

"Okay." He started walking again. "Not what I expected, but glad to have a heads up."

Only a few doors down, Morgan stopped again. His gaze went from the sign in the yard to the open front door, up the almost three story high columns and back. Another moment and a young guy the size of an NFL linebacker came out the door carrying a large box with the same ease Valerie would carry a bag of potato chips.

"Morning." The linebacker waved, somehow juggling the huge package with only one hand.

"I see you're selling." Morgan pointed at the sign.

"Not me. My mom. Well, actually my grandmother. She's held onto this old house since forever, but none of us want anything this big, so Mom and she agreed it's time."

"Wayne, don't forget to bring me the empty boxes from the car." A slim woman with salt and pepper hair, wearing the West Texas uniform of jeans and cowboy boots, smiled at the linebacker then turned her attention to Valerie and Morgan. "Good morning!"

"Morning." Morgan tipped his hat. "It's a nice house."

"I think so." She looked up and over her shoulder at the expansive columns. "Want to take a look inside?"

The first thing that hadn't stopped surprising Valerie was how friendly strangers were around here. The second thing that got her was the twinkle in Morgan's eyes that brought memories of the Christmas morning gleam in her nephew's eyes.

"Thank you, ma'am. That would be very nice."

And everyone using "ma'am" was the third thing she hadn't gotten used to yet.

At the top of the steps, Morgan held out his hand. "Morgan Farraday. Nice to meet you."

"You're not one of Brian's boys, are you?"

Morgan shook his head. "No, ma'am. Patrick."

"Ah. Haven't seen much of Patrick since his wife got on her high horse and rode out of town." The woman turned for the door and then stopped and spun around. "No offense intended. She was a lovely woman."

"Yes, ma'am." Morgan nodded and followed the woman into the house, then stepped aside to wave Valerie in first.

A girl could really get used to all this cowboy chivalry.

"It's time to downsize. The family is so spread out that I don't even get a full house for Thanksgiving anymore. Seems silly to trudge through keeping up for just me."

"You're the grandmother?" Valerie didn't mean to sound so surprised, but except for the graying hair, she looked much too young to be the grandmother of the linebacker.

The woman laughed. "I'll take that as a compliment."

"You must have been really young when you started having a family." Valerie couldn't get over how much this woman could pass for her own mother.

"I was thirty-two when I had my Benny. Thirty-five when Wayne's mama was born."

Val did some fast math and realized the lady had to be at least seventy-five. Maybe there was more to be said for this West Texas living, cowboy boots and all.

"It needs a little work." The woman picked up a box from the corner of the entry. Standing tall, her smile bright, her gaze reflected the pride she held in her home. "Not as bad as some of the abandoned homes you find in these parts, but not as pristine as when Herbert and I bought it."

Morgan ran his fingers down the wood trim. "Nice craftsmanship."

"That's because it was built at a time when people actually took pride in their work. Despite their age, not a single wall is out of plumb. Even brand-spanking new homes seem to have a hard time understanding the concept of plumb and level."

"Don't I know that." Inching forward, he glanced into the first room to his left.

"I need to bring these upstairs." She juggled two large empty boxes. "Feel free to walk around."

Valerie followed him into the first room. The layout reminded her a bit of Meg's. "This is bigger than it looks from the outside."

"All these historical homes are deceiving in the perception of size."

They walked through another room, probably what was once a formal dining room. From there, they looped through the kitchen. Most likely updated a few times in its history. She'd guess the last time had been at least 30 or so years ago, or however long ago honey oak cabinets were popular. Coming around to the opposite side of the house, having followed a U shaped pattern, she heard Morgan's sharp intake of breath when he crossed the next threshold.

"Is something wrong?"

He stepped to the side, allowing her to enter the room first. "Just didn't expect to find this. So many people pull out the paneling and shelving in original libraries in order to make them into a den, media room, playroom for the kids, or whatever current incarnation is needed for a modern family."

She snapped her jaw shut at the sight of floor to ceiling bookshelves and pointed up. "It even has a brass railing for a rolling ladder." Quickly she glanced around the room in search of the ladder or some remnants of one, but found nothing.

"Sure looks like it." His gaze made the same trip hers had, most likely in search of the ladder as well.

Taking in the expansive empty shelves, she gently touched one of the wooden planks. "Ever since I was a little girl and watched the movie *My Fair Lady* with my mom, I've always thought how cool it would be to have a library like Professor Higgins."

"Really?" His gaze leveled with hers. "I wouldn't have pictured you as a grand library kind of girl. No offense meant."

"None taken."

"For me, it was an insurance commercial filmed at the old library at Fordham University in New York."

"Alumni?"

"Not this Oklahoma boy." He chuckled. "The wonders of the modern Internet. It was pretty easy to do a search and get the answer. It was a pretty cool commercial."

"Do you have a library where you live now?" she asked.

He shook his head. "No. Dad's office has some shelves and some books, but it's more of a man cave than a library. What about you?"

"Afraid not." She tipped her head and shrugged a single shoulder. "Reading material and high-pressure television industry don't seem to be conducive to each other."

"I don't know about that. Some people might say the same thing about ranchers and reading material."

She shrugged her shoulder and crinkled then smoothed her forehead. "What kind of books would you fill this room with?"

"That's easy." He grinned. "Everything."

"Everything?"

He nodded. "Why, do you have something in particular in mind?"

"Actually, I like biographies. I love learning the truth in history. When I find the time to binge a little TV, I can spend hours going down the digital rabbit hole comparing the past with the televised presentation of it. Mysteries are fun sometimes. Especially the cozies. Probably had the love of amateur sleuths ingrained in me from watching Jessica Fletcher solve crimes in Cabot Cove every Sunday night like clockwork. But over there," she pointed to the wall behind him, "I would fill every last one of those shelves with my favorite romance novels."

His gaze followed her finger from ceiling to floor and back. "That's a lot of romance."

"It is. A girl can never have too many comfortable shoes, too many friends, or too many good books."

"That seems like a sound philosophy. Though, you're always in heels?"

Her hands flipped up in a 'so what' gesture. "Who says they're not comfortable?"

"My mistake." He smiled.

She knew he didn't believe her, and she'd already made a mental note to make time to call some of those friends she hadn't spoken to in eons, but her mind was once again shifting gears. "I wonder how hard it would be to replace the ladder."

"Not very."

It took her a moment to realize Morgan was mentally measuring, calculating, and most likely, restoring the beautiful old room in his mind. "I hope the right person gets this place. Despite my line of work, even I'd hate to see it relegated to a bland media room for ill-tempered teens."

Morgan's head bobbed and Neil's voice drifted across the main hall.

"In here." Morgan continued looking at the upper shelves in the room.

"Ready when you are?" Neil leaned against the doorway and whistled. "Sweet. You taking on bidding now?"

Morgan shook his head from side to side. "Nope, that's still Owen's job. Just a little personal curiosity."

"Well, I'm personally curious about Three Corners, so let's head out." Neil stepped away from the doorway, giving Morgan and Val plenty of space to lead the way to the street.

Hand on the doorknob, she looked over her shoulder at the expansive stairway leading to the second floor. Once upon a time, this must have been one hell of a house.

"It really could have waited until tomorrow." A tray of warm biscuits in one hand, Meg shoved the oven door shut with the other. "But I admit, it was a bit of a thrill to walk into the room a bit ago and see it all painted one beautiful color."

As if agreeing, Fiona banged her hands on the tray and grinned.

"See. Even Fiona loves the color."

"Personally," Adam pulled several glasses out of the cupboard, "I think she's just happy to get a biscuit."

Meg shot her husband a tight-lipped glare not intended for the general public and Adam shrugged, smiled, and kissed her cheek as he walked past her, instantly melting the icy gaze.

"As I was saying," Meg continued, "we all love it. Thank you."

"On that I can definitely agree." Adam set a glass in front of each cousin. "Thank you."

"It really was our pleasure." Neil bobbed his head and waved a thumb at his brother. "Though I guess mostly his and Ryan's since they did most of the work."

"You put in your share this morning." Meg slid the butter tray in front of them. "Credit given where credit's due."

"Yes, Ma'am." Neil didn't dare argue.

"So," Adam pulled a seat up next to the baby's high chair, "do we know how much longer before Valerie can join us?"

"All she said when she walked out of the kitchen this afternoon was *Don't hold dinner*." Meg set the pot of beef stew in front of Morgan. "Do either of you have any idea what that's all about?"

"Maybe," Neil said.

"Or maybe not." Morgan hadn't quite figured out how they'd gotten roped into whatever it was they'd agreed to do.

"English please?" Adam blew on a piece of biscuit for his daughter.

"Funny," Morgan put his napkin on his lap, "that's what I was thinking the whole time Valerie was talking."

"From what I can tell," Neil reached for salt, "she needs to do something called a sizzle reel."

"Unless it's got something to do with steak, that could be alarming." Adam cut up a piece of stew meat to set on Fiona's plate.

Morgan reached for his fork. "It's a short video. I think Valerie said about six minutes. It's what's used in the business to sell a television idea."

"I thought that's what pilots are for?" Meg pulled her seat in on the other side of her daughter.

"That comes after," Morgan said.

"After the sizzle reel?" Meg looked his way.

"Exactly." That part Morgan had followed fine. It was what came next that still had him scratching his head. "And we're going to be the...uh...actors."

"The what?" Adam almost dropped his fork.

"Not exactly actors," Neil corrected. "From what Val explained, a sizzle reel can be thrown together with stock images and shorts to create a visual presentation. She feels that her idea will sell better if she can do live footage of the town."

"So where do you two come in?" Meg handed Fiona her sippy cup.

"Like I said," Morgan put his fork down, "acting. The whole premise is one of those reality renovation television shows. Which requires your key renovators."

"You two?" Adam's voice dripped with something akin to disbelief.

"Not us specifically," Neil answered. "More of a stand in. She needs a couple of professionals who look the part." He smiled proudly. "So we volunteered."

"*You* volunteered." Morgan skewered his brother with a sharp glare. "Somewhere between telling her what a lovely smile she had, and just about drooling over the delicious steakhouse in Butler Springs you clearly plan to invite her to, you volunteered *all* available Farradays to play fixer upper."

Adam's head shot up. "*All*? And available for what?"

Neil stabbed at a potato and held his fork midair. "I was referring to the Oklahoma Farradays, or in this case, the Farraday cousins as we're referred to around town."

"Valerie didn't seem very sure how long it was going to take her to get a production crew out here. She seemed to think her chances of snagging a Dallas crew were better than Albuquerque, but whatever the resolution, we Farradays, at least for now, are her cast."

"Well, isn't that fun?" Meg grinned up at him.

Fun was not the word that came to the front of his mind. The idea of working with Val held a certain appeal, but not so much the idea of doing it in front of a camera.

"In college I took a few performing arts classes." Neil looked to Meg. "Mostly set building and the like for my portfolio, but I got a chance or two to get up on stage." Turning to face his brother, he continued, "It could be a lot of fun."

"I did it!" Hands clasped high in front of her Valerie bounced into the large kitchen. "I'll have a full crew here tomorrow and we'll film the day after."

"Full crew?" Meg asked hesitantly.

"Not as many as we'll have when we're shooting for the season, but enough to get some choice footage. Then it'll go off to my editors in LA. Ooh." Val spotted the stew in everyone's dishes. "I love beef stew. Didn't realize how hungry I was till this very minute."

"There's plenty." Meg jumped up from her seat.

"No." Valerie waved her back. "I've got it."

Retrieving a bowl from the spot saved for her at the

massive island, Valerie walked over to the stove and filled her dish. She was rambling on about her ideas, scenes she hoped to shoot, things she hoped to see, something about the sisters and their brothel, but most of it faded away as he watched her move about the kitchen. Nothing about the woman in faded jeans, the requisite Texas cowboy boots, and that pretty scarf now tying her hair back in a floppy ponytail bore any resemblance to the woman he'd met in the café just a few short days ago. She seemed as much at ease in the kitchen as she might be on a Hollywood runway, and as enthused about interacting with a baby as filming her next idea. How much more was there to Valerie Moore?

CHAPTER NINE

Valerie had to call in more than a few favors to pull off her plan. To do the shoot right, to get what she wanted, she needed plenty of cameras and about four days. Then she'd need a couple of weeks for edit. That of course would be done back in LA. It had taken most of the other afternoon and the better part of the next morning to bring everything completely together.

It had taken a bit longer to convince the sisters there was no such thing as ghosts, crying for help or otherwise. After she'd succeeded in her efforts, the two women finally agreed to let the production crew camp out in the old brothel. With the long hours she'd expected the shoot to take, and the long drive in and out of town, she decided to stay at the restored brothel as well.

Val sniffed the air. "Coffee smells heavenly."

Whichever of the sisters was the blonde with hair as high as she was wide, grinned from behind the makeshift breakfast bar. "Sissy has always made a mean cup of coffee."

Hoping the morning brew tasted as good as it smelled, Val poured herself a cup and nodded.

"Did you sleep well?" the blonde squeaked out.

For a fraction of a moment Val was tempted to tell the older woman that she couldn't get a wink of sleep thanks to all the sounds of chains rattling in her room, but the nervous anticipation on the blonde's face kept Val from teasing her. "Slept like a log. The mattresses on those beds are very comfortable. You guys did great."

Sister's smile brightened. "Oh, I'm so glad to hear that. Sissy will be delighted too."

"Where is Sissy?"

"She's helping set up the food tables outside. I know your schedule said things would be starting early today and we wanted to be ready."

From all the activity up and down the hall already this morning, she knew her crew was up and judging from the empty lobby, most likely outside and ready to get started. What she hadn't counted on was stepping outside the door and finding half the town showing up for the shoot as well.

"Oh, this is so exciting!" the tall redheaded sister squealed with way too much enthusiasm for this hour of the morning. "We have more coffee and lemonade and sweet tea…"

Valerie tried really hard not to shudder at the thought of all that sweetness. In the south, sweet tea wasn't just iced tea with a little sugar, it was more like sugar with a little tea.

Eileen stood beside the redheaded sister. Once Val had realized getting a food truck of any kind to come out to the isolated location would be next to impossible, Eileen Farraday had been one of the first to volunteer to keep the food and drinks flowing. So many residents were thrilled with the whole project that the town had arranged for enough food to feed a Hollywood movie crew rather than a small sizzle reel crew. Of course, she hadn't considered they would be feeding the crew and the audience.

A donut clenched between his teeth, a cameraman walked past her to the morning shoot. One by one other crew members followed, setting up equipment to check light and sound.

"Is there a hot sheet?" one of the team asked.

Valerie shook her head and pointed to the one side of the old emporium. "I want a camera here." Her finger turned to the upper corner of the interior. "And here." She turned. "We're going to mostly run it and gun it."

"Do I want to know what that means?" Eileen mumbled quietly.

Val bit back a laugh. "This won't be scripted so we're just going to have as many cameras as possible shooting whatever construction action there is and hope that we get something worth turning into a TV show."

"Where's the peach cobbler?" The woman with a braid that hung all the way down her back, Ruth maybe, frowned at the table in front of her.

"I put it on the…corner." Eileen stepped away from her table and walking to the food spread, stopped only a few feet away. "I know I put it there."

"Maybe someone on the crew took it." Sister frowned.

Valerie lowered her gaze. "The whole thing?"

"We're ready," one of the camera men called out from the emporium doorway.

"Have to run, ladies." Val needed to give the cameramen a list of shots she was hoping to get.

By lunchtime they'd captured several great candid moments but nothing quite fit the vision in her head. Except maybe for Morgan with a tool belt on his hips. Who knew worn leather, and with a measuring tape clipped to the side, could look so good. His brothers didn't look half bad either. Even if Neil didn't normally swing a hammer but instead his tool of choice was a pencil, the man would have the female fans drooling nonetheless.

"Oh, hell." Neil stepped back and a lifted board snapped heavily into place. "We're going to have to watch our step. At least some of these floorboards have broken free."

The camera zoomed in as he pushed on the edge of the board with his booted foot and the opposite end flipped up and then down again. Maybe if one of those floorboards had whacked a brother in the butt that would have made for interesting footage. This was proving harder than she'd anticipated. Who knew renovations could be so boring.

"Hey, fellas?" Maybe she could come up with anything to spark some interest in this otherwise boring project. Looking at one of the cameramen, she ran her thumb across her neck, signaling them to stop their taping. She started across the shop with no idea what to do or say, but with any luck, once she got in the thick of things she was hoping some brilliant and slightly different twist would occur to her. "What if we try…"

The words were barely out of her mouth when her

balance abandoned ship and she flailed like a gasping fish tossed on an old dock. As the wooden floorboard she'd stepped on fell out from under her, her arms continued circling around and a thought flashed through her mind—too bad she'd ordered the cameras to stop rolling. If there was one thing people enjoyed watching, it was slapstick. And her crashing on her well-padded derriere would have been fabulous footage.

"Hey!" Like an eagle swooping in to steal its floundering prey, strong arms curled around her and scooped her against a rock solid wall of man. "Are you okay?"

Pressed against Morgan, she could feel his heart thumping under her splayed fingertips and wasn't sure whose rapid beat was faster. "Fine. Uh, thank you."

"You need to watch your step on a construction site. Can't take anything for granted."

She nodded her head and resisted the urge to tighten her arms around his neck.

"Great shot." One of the cameramen came running up beside her. "You were right. The extra cameras on the run it and gun it paid off."

It took her a few moments to realize what the man was talking about. Kicking her feet, she pushed away from Morgan until he released his hold and easing her down, she found her footing. "You filmed my falling?"

"Two cameras got the carpenter coming to the rescue. You can thank us for not shutting down later." The sandy haired cameraman stared pointedly at her, then turned and walked away.

At least she hadn't been in heels and a dress or she might have really made a fool of herself. Casually brushing the dust and embarrassment away, she pressed on with the day. They had a long way to go still.

Back to work, Valerie's gaze drifted from the beautiful shiplap walls to the growing pile of planks on the floor. "Do you really have to remove all those boards?"

"This is the twenty-first century. We know a thing or two more about insulation now. We'll add some two by sixes, install the insulation, and replace the shiplap. Nobody will ever know what happened, and no one will freeze in the dead of winter."

"This is Texas. How cold could it get?"

Morgan smiled. "This is *West* Texas. And *very* cold."

"Don't get too carried away. This is only a sizzle. If it doesn't get picked up for a pilot, we won't be able to fix up what you've dismantled." She glanced briefly at the bare wall. This had better be the best darn sizzle reel she'd ever produced, because if it didn't get picked up, she was just plain out of ideas.

Every single minute of the day Morgan asked himself how did he let himself get talked into this. Every minute *except* the one where Valerie folded into his arms and against his chest. Neil and Ryan were both getting into the strutting peacock thing, but Morgan was thinking it would be nice to go back and do a slow motion replay of the part where he scooped her into his arms—and keep her there. Then again, reality never turned out as well as the dream. Which is why he reminded himself it was safer not to dream at all.

"What are you stewing over?" Neil spun his hammer the way an old gunslinger might twirl a revolver, then slipped it into the tool loop.

"You've been watching too many westerns." Ryan shook his head.

Neil shrugged. "Don't you feel it?"

"Feel it?" Morgan asked.

"You know. The vibe."

"The vibe?" Ryan repeated.

"What? Did you two have parrot soup for lunch or something? The old west vibe, the feeling that we're living over a hundred years ago." Neil glanced at the one camera still rolling and pulled the pocket knife from his pouch, then lowered his voice. "I can see where that camera could begin to feel like being under a microscope."

Morgan shook his head. That's what he'd been saying from the first time the words reality television were spoken in conjunction with Three Corners and his brothers. Pocket knife in hand, he joined his brother splitting open the rolls of insulation. Normally they would do work in sections, remove the boards first, then install insulation, then recover the walls. In this case they agreed they would work in small sections so that things were not in disarray when the work had to stop.

"I've always wondered why insulation is pink." Hands on her hips, Valerie looked at the unrolled sheets of insulation. "Personally, I prefer purple."

She reached for the insulation and Morgan snatched hold of her wrist. "Careful. You have to wear gloves to handle it. Fiberglass is seriously itchy."

"Poison ivy itchy," Neil added.

"Here." Morgan pulled his spare gloves out of a bucket. "You want to help?"

"Sure." She smiled. "Why not?"

"Paper side faces out."

"Out. Got it." She grabbed hold of a piece, looked up, and to his surprise, tucked the bottom edge in between the new studs and pressed it into place from the bottom up. At one point the pink fluff was draped over her head and down her back as she straightened, pushing it into place. Her arms stretched up high, the top edge flopped over her hands and she pushed onto her tiptoes. "I need longer arms."

"Let me help," three voices tumbled over each other as each brother made a short leap to help. Neil accidentally hip checked Ryan. Ryan spun out of the way and bumped into Morgan, and before he could catch his balance, he fell into Valerie. The four of them toppled over, bringing the long swaths of insulation with them.

Valerie didn't even try to hide her giggles as she clawed her way out from under the massive pink fuzzy strip. "I don't think it's supposed to work this way."

Sitting on his rear, Ryan chuckled and shook his head. "Nope."

Morgan agreed. "Can't say I've ever seen it done quite this way before."

"Maybe," Neil's eyes twinkled under raised brows, "you shouldn't help."

"Let me." Morgan lifted the remainder of the strip of insulation away and tucked it all the way into the wall.

From across the way, one of the cameramen slowly approached with a slight limp. "You okay, Ted? You seem to be favoring one foot."

"Just a bit. Tripped over a rogue footstool."

Val tipped her head sideways. "Rogue?"

The cameraman shrugged a shoulder and aimed his thumb at one of the other production people. "Mike thought rearranging the furniture in the middle of the night was an entertaining past time."

"I heard that." Mike's voice boomed from outside the doorway. "And I told you, the stepstool was not in the middle of the floor when I went to bed last night. You probably just weren't watching where you were walking."

"Rather hard to see your way to the bathroom without any light. All I know is someone, or something, moved the stepstool and my little toe still stings."

"There you go, talking things going bump in the night again."

The cameraman took a step back and held his free hand up. "Just reporting the facts. And the fact is, my little toe hurts like the dickens."

Val waved her fingers at the two men. "Just don't let the sisters hear you or we'll never get this shot finished."

"The sisters?" Morgan repeated. "What do they have to do with any of this?"

"They think the place is haunted. Poppycock. I say we forget about stepstools and grab a snack."

Ryan unsnapped his belt. "Works for me. There's a whoopee pie out there with my name on it."

"I'm not sure I want to know what that is." Neil lay his belt down on the counter beside Ryan's.

"You need to come to town more often." Morgan followed his brother's lead. "Toni makes them. It's a New England staple. Basically cream filled chocolate cake cookies."

"Did someone say chocolate cake?" Val looked from one brother to the other. "I have a weakness for anything chocolate."

"Then you should taste her Boston Cream pie. "I've never had anything like it."

Val grinned up at him. "That I've had. Great snack shack at Logan Airport. I could have eaten my way through the place."

"I wonder what'll be for dinner?" Neck stretched, Ryan searched ahead to the food tables.

"Do you ever stop eating?" Morgan asked his brother. Lunch had been a delicious brisket with the traditional cole slaw and potato salad sides. As expected, there was enough to feed an army. "How can you even consider dinner after the lunch we had?"

"What can I say?" Ryan shrugged then flashed a toothy grin. "I'm a growing boy."

One by one, his brothers slid their requisite cowboy hat onto their heads. Val followed suit, doing the same with the hat Toni had given her. In only a few days, she'd really grown into the part. From the top of her Stetson right down to the tips of her cowboy boots. Side by side with his brothers, Morgan had come to at least one conclusion: Valerie Moore may not know it, but she was meant to be in cattle country West Texas.

CHAPTER TEN

"These last few days have been such a trip, watching how Hollywood really works." Joanna Farraday placed a barbecued rib on her plate. "This has been seriously beyond fun."

The last day of shooting for the sizzle reel was now finished, and the town surprised Valerie and the crew with a wrap party. Everyone was so excited; she didn't have the heart to tell them that Hollywood didn't throw parties for sizzle reels. Besides, she was starting to understand it was more than just acres and acres of cattle that made Texas so famous for its barbecue. If the stuff tasted half as good as it smelled, the food was going to be out of this world.

"Fun's one word for it." One of the Dallas crew standing in line shook his head. "I for one am glad to be heading home tonight."

Val glanced down at her watch. "At this hour?" The drive to Dallas would take the better part of a day.

Another crew member behind her shook his head. "Don't mind him. Ted's never had a curious soul."

"Curious?" Ted dropped a spoonful of potato salad on his dish. "Try creepy."

"Creepy?" Valerie repeated.

"A few odd things happen and Ted's all freaked out."

"A few?" Ted turned to his crewmate. "Your walls weren't talking to you all night."

"I keep telling you," his buddy rolled his eyes, "they were just weird dreams. I didn't hear a thing."

"Dreams my…" he quickly glanced at the two women staring at him and cleared his throat, "dreams my foot."

"What are all the serious faces for?" Morgan joined the

line. "Y'all are supposed to be having a good time."

"This is just the start." Eileen strolled up, grinning. She had on an ankle length gingham skirt and plain white cotton top. Valerie didn't remember ever seeing the woman in anything but the standard rancher's uniform: blue jeans and boots. Eileen lifted her chin across the road toward the old saloon. "We ladies have been spit and polishing the place all day. The real fun starts after everyone eats."

Not till this moment had Valerie realized all the folks coming and going from the saloon. Some folks from the line ahead of her were carrying their full plates inside the old building, a few men were carrying cases inside, and others were coming out empty-handed, but all moving with purpose to a large truck she hadn't noticed before.

"Just the same," Ted smiled at Eileen, "I'll be getting on the road after dinner, but thank you very much for your hospitality. It's been an...interesting gig."

Brows curved into a deep V, Eileen watched the man walk over to the saloon before turning to Valerie. "Something going on I should know about?"

His buddy grabbed a napkin and blew out a sigh. "Ted just spooks easy. So what if someone filled the sugar bowl with salt. Mistakes like that happen all the time."

"When was this?" Eileen's frown remained firmly in place.

"Yesterday." He shrugged. "Poor sisters were all a flutter. Neither could explain how it happened since no one fessed up to touching the sugar bowls. Ted was already spooked by the moving furniture and voices in the walls."

Eileen looked from him to Val and back. "I didn't hear anything about that."

"It's a first for me too." Valerie shrugged. "I suppose we're lucky Ted didn't hear women screaming for help or we might have lost ourselves one cameraman and wound up running behind schedule." She didn't even want to think about how much more that would add to the cost of this little venture.

"What do you mean, moving furniture?" Eileen asked.

The other crewman reached for a biscuit. "It started the

first night. Ted's a tall guy so he didn't need the stepstool to climb into bed. He moved it out of the way to the foot of the bed and settled in for the night. Well, the next morning he tripped over the dumb thing as it was back to where it had been set originally. I figure he just forgot he didn't move it, but he keeps insisting if Mike the crew prankster didn't move it, then it reappeared all by itself."

Eileen kept her gaze on him. When he continued loading his plate, she prompted him, "You said started?"

"Yep. Following day, after work finished up, he went upstairs and all the furniture in his room had been flipped around. This time he figured the sisters were just keeping busy redecorating. This morning when he thanked the two women for moving the bed away from the window, he discovered they'd had nothing to do with it. That on top of yesterday's incident with the sugar bowl and the salt, and the voices he insisted weren't dreams, he's convinced the place is haunted."

"Well, that's just ridiculous." Eileen hefted one fist on her hip. "Anybody else agree with him?"

The crewmen hesitated before shrugging casually. "The possibility occurred to a few of us. But there's always an explanation. My guess is someone on the crew knew Ted was spooked by forgetting about the footstool and they decided to play a practical joke on him. I'm sure eventually someone will fess up about rearranging his room. And no offense meant to either sister, but they seemed kind of flustered on more than one occasion. It's also not hard to see somebody pouring salt into the sugar bowl and not remembering." His plate piled high with just about everything the townsfolk had brought for the potluck celebration, the crewman dipped his head. "If you'll excuse me."

Eileen nodded and grabbed her own plate. "I'm surprised, as spooked as the sisters were earlier this year about the brothel being haunted, that they didn't say something to me about this."

"They were pretty upset about that screaming woman, but they didn't say anything about moving furniture and seasoning switches." Valerie did not need rumors of the place being haunted getting around or this whole project could blow up in her face. No, she did not need that at all.

The low murmur of chatter in the small saloon gave way to the melodic sounds of live music coming from outside. Folks had been eating and chatting and moving about from table to table in the old saloon while Ned played the old piano. Who knew the old coot could tickle the ivories with the same skill as he wielded a socket wrench. Several of the Farradays—including Morgan—and the Bradys had come together while folks were eating to set up the wooden platform out in the street.

The last hour or so Morgan had sat with his family but kept an eye on Valerie. He'd done a lot of that the last few days. For a big city girl, she had more country in her than he would have expected.

"Looks like the party is moving outside." Aunt Eileen pushed away from the table. She and the other Farraday wives had gotten together and dressed for the evening in long skirts and pinned up hair in homage to the days when the old town was still thriving. Not exactly period pieces but a festive touch.

Joanna Farraday stood and pushed her seat up to the table. "We should do this more often. It's kind of fun to dress up."

"I know." Hannah patted at the bun atop her head. "I may start wearing skirts more often. They're way more comfortable than I expected."

"Until you have to go to the bathroom." Catherine pushed in her chair and picked up her drink. "Pulling down jeans is much easier than gathering up layers of a long skirt."

"Okay, ladies. TMI." Morgan was pretty easy going, but some subjects were better ignored.

"Agreed." Connor kissed his wife's temple and

extended his arm to her. "Shall we?"

"Why, I'd be delighted." Batting her lashes at her husband, Catherine's pitch was a tad higher and sweeter than usual.

Following his family outside, Morgan casually glanced about, searching for Valerie. Between her crew and all the folks from town eager to visit with her, she'd been kept busy all through dinner. He wasn't even sure if she'd gotten a chance to sit down and eat.

"Oh my." Aunt Eileen slowed her steps. "I do believe everybody outdid themselves. If I didn't know better, I swear I was standing in the 1800s on a Saturday night."

Checkered tablecloths covered a line of tables heavy with desserts. One looked more delicious than the next. Strands of overhead lights hung from building to building over the large wooden dance area center of the street. To one side, an elevated platform held the small band already playing a rhythmic tune. The fiddler in the forefront had bystanders gathered, tapping their toes.

"Shall we?" Sean Faraday bowed at the waist and extended his hand to his wife.

Morgan made another quick scan of the area as the dance floor grew more crowded. His efforts were rewarded when he spotted Valerie talking to the sisters by the punchbowl. Trying not to look like an overeager teen, he leisurely made his way up the street as quickly as possible. "So far the party looks like a booming success."

Both Sister and Sissy beamed at him, but Sissy was almost giddy with delight. "I am so glad Valerie talked us into participating in this. I do hope that we can bring this town back to life."

Sister bobbed her head. "There is something to be said for stepping back in time. This town could be a wonderful learning tool for children. It's no Versailles, but I think it's worth preserving."

"Most definitely," Valerie agreed.

"If you ladies would excuse us," he turned to face Valerie, "may I have the honor of the first dance?"

"Oh yes," one sister squealed. "You two hurry off." The

two sisters were as different as night and day—one tall one short, one blonde one redhead, one always laughing the other a little more serious—but tonight both were clearly in seventh heaven.

Delighted for a legitimate excuse to hold her hand, Morgan led Valerie onto the dance floor. "You look absolutely lovely this evening."

"Thank you. When some of the ladies mentioned dressing up for tonight in somewhat period costume, I have to admit, I got a little bit giddy. Dress-up was my favorite thing to play as a little girl. I loved watching old movies. Really old movies. The ones from the thirties, forties or fifties where women wore gorgeous gowns, fabulous hats, elegant hairdos, and shoes to die for."

That would certainly explain her strong fashion sense when she first came to town. Striking, and very attractive.

"I suppose that make-believe world is what drew me into show business."

"Did you ever want to be an actor?"

"Not really. I used to read a lot. I loved going to new places without leaving my room. Mom got me started watching old movies. She loved the musicals. We'd have oldies movie nights for us and action adventure with Dad. You might say I have very well-rounded taste. In the end, everything related to the big screen fascinated me, right down the lighting and the editing. I could praise or criticize a film better than the motion picture academy."

She said that with so much pride it made him chuckle.

"By the time I got to college, I figured I might as well work in a field I loved. By graduation, I'd gone from the big screen to the small screen, and instead of creating new worlds somehow I wound up recreating reality." The last few words came out almost bitterly before her face brightened. "Does it count that as a kid I wanted to be Ginger Rogers dancing with Fred Astaire?"

"I don't dance anywhere near as well as Fred, but Ginger can't hold a candle to you." He twirled her in place and pulled her into his embrace.

"Thank you, and you dance very well."

"My mother convinced me at an early age that all the girls liked the boy who knew how to dance."

"Your mother sounds like a smart woman."

"Maybe not about everything, but she was certainly right about dancing."

Valerie chuckled. "In other words, you got all the girls."

"Not all." He twirled her again. He paused another beat before adding, "But I was never left standing alone at a school dance."

"I bet you weren't." She remained quiet a long minute. "Who was she?"

"She?"

"The one who broke your heart."

"I didn't say anyone broke my heart."

"You didn't have to. Friendly, good looking, and smart man like you is still single. Only one possible explanation. The one who wouldn't dance must have broken your heart."

He actually found himself smiling. And when did thinking of Carolyn come with a smile instead of the bitter taste of soured memories. "Her name was Carolyn. She taught me a valuable lesson."

"What was that?"

"Sometimes giving one hundred percent isn't enough. Some people always want more."

"Sounds like the wrong fit."

Too bad he hadn't figured that out a whole lot sooner. Carolyn had been everything he'd thought he wanted. Beautiful, friendly and smart. Good to friends and family, she shared his values. At least he thought she did. What took him too long to see was the prestige that came with his family ranch and construction business was firmly rooted in Oklahoma country, and Carolyn's dreams were firmly rooted in plans to move up to bigger and better places. Last he'd heard, she married a guy whose ranch had oil. They spent most of their time in Houston and the rest in those famous big cities she always talked about. "Let's just say not every one is cut out to be half of a happy couple."

"Ouch. That sounds rather cynical."

"And safe."

"You didn't strike me as the kind of man afraid to take risks."

"There's a difference between high risk and a suicide mission. There's a lot to be said for playing it safe." Though right now, playing with fire held a great deal of appeal, even at the risk of getting burned. Again.

"I don't know. Sometimes safe can be pretty boring."

"Since I doubt Hollywood is ever boring, would I be guessing correctly that's the other reason you chose show business?"

"Probably."

All the more reason to wonder why she was so hell bent on selling an idea that would keep her in boring West Texas. The first notes of a familiar country song began playing and the couples immediately began gliding along in a fast-moving circle.

"Oh my." Valerie stepped on his foot, glancing left and right at the uniformly moving crowd.

His hand on her hip he guided her. "The Texas Two Step is a lot like walking, only quick quick then slow slow."

Once more she bumped into his foot before falling into the rhythm. "Oh, this is easy."

"Very. It's why the dance is so popular." Once they'd made a few turns around the floor with the growing crowd, he spun her about, pleased to see her fall easily back into step again. "There you go. You've got it."

"This is fun."

"Just like walking to music."

"I like that. Walking to music." She added a little bounce to her step. "Like life—or relationships—sometimes it's easy, sometimes you trip, but if you don't give up, it can simply be fun."

"What happens now?"

"I guess that depends on the next song."

"I mean now that the reel is done."

"I've already sent it off to editing in LA. That could take as long as a couple of weeks. Then we'll pitch it and if all goes well, a pilot will be ordered, and then if all goes the way I think it will, we'll be back again to film a series."

"How soon are you leaving?"

The bounce in her steps slid away. "There's no reason to stay really."

His jaw tightened and he nodded. Sometimes you trip, sometimes you fall, and sometimes there's no point in getting back up.

CHAPTER ELEVEN

"I can't believe you ladies are here playing cards bright and early after last night." Donna, a longtime waitress at the cafe, poured more coffee into Eileen Farraday's mug.

"You were there too." Ruth Ann tossed a chip into the pot. "I'm in."

Donna circled the table to refill Dorothy's cup. "Yes, I was there, but I didn't close the place down. Like Cinderella and her pumpkin, I was home in bed shortly after midnight. I heard you ladies were still cutting a rug into the wee hours of this morning."

Sally May set her cards down. "I'm out. And I'd hardly call two-thirty the wee hours."

"Absolutely." Eileen folded her cards and tossed a chip in the pot. "Maybe four o'clock would be wee hours. In New York the bars close down at four in the morning, then we'd all head out for breakfast. But nobody can eat breakfast at 3 o'clock in the morning, so that's just a very late night."

"Even Abbie didn't come in this morning." Smiling, Donna blew out a short sigh. "When I grow up I want to have a constitution like y'all."

"Atta girl." Dorothy flipped a chip into the pot. "What the hey, I'll call."

"Read 'em and weep." Ruth Ann laid down a royal flush.

Dorothy shook her head. "With a hand like that you should have bet more."

"If I'd have bet more all of you would have folded."

"Maybe." Eileen shrugged, then looked around. From

the looks of things pretty much everyone else in town was sleeping in too. Nonetheless, leaning forward she lowered her voice. "I had a long chitchat with Gray before I got in the truck."

Ruth Ann stopped shuffling her cards. "You *what*?"

"You heard me. I kept watching Valerie and Morgan most of the night."

"I know." Dorothy smiled. "They do make a lovely couple."

Eileen waved a hand in the air. "What good is that if she's on the West Coast and he's here? From the conversation at breakfast this morning, it doesn't sound like they've made any plans to talk to each other, never mind see each other, once she goes back to California."

Slipping the deck to her side for Sally May to cut, Ruth Ann huffed at her friend. "Did it occur to you that maybe he didn't think their plans were any of your business?"

"Nonsense. No reason to hide anything from me. Besides, I came right out and asked if he'd be talking to her again."

Dorothy frowned slightly. "And he said no?"

"Isn't that what I just said?" Eileen leaned back in her chair. "So getting into the truck, I called Gray over. Asked him outright was he positive that Morgan and Valerie were meant to be."

Sally May picked up her first card and glanced sideways at Eileen. "What did he say?"

"Would you listen to yourselves." Ruth Ann continued dealing. "Our dog doesn't talk."

"Maybe not in words like you and me, but trust me, that dog communicates when he wants to." Sally May picked up another card.

"She's right." Eileen placed her hand on the back of her cards.

"So what did he say?"

"He tipped his head one way as I talked, looked off to the horizon, and as sure as I am that my name is Eileen Farraday, that dog sat back on his haunches, lifted his head, gave a single bark, then bouncing up and wagging his tail, licked my hand before running off with the men to work the cattle."

"Maybe he was just saying good morning," Dorothy suggested.

"Or maybe," Sally May waved a thumb at her longtime friend, "the dog knows something we don't."

"Won't be the first time." Dorothy picked up her cards.

So far those dogs were ten for ten with the Farraday offspring. Even the most unlikely of matches. Eileen didn't have a clue how this was going to work out but she had faith in Gray and his cohort.

"Good morning," Ruth Ann announced a little more loudly than necessary, unless...

Eileen craned her neck and spotted Valerie coming to a stop beside her. "Joining us for a game?"

"Meg said that an invite to join the poker game was a rare thing not to be missed. Besides, I never was any good at sleeping in after the sun is up."

"Sounds like you'd have made a good rancher." Eileen scooted her chair over. "Most of them are up long before the sun anyhow."

Sally May kicked Eileen under the table and skewered her with a keep your mouth shut glare.

"I can't imagine being a rancher." Val settled into the seat between Eileen and Sally May.

"You can't?" Dorothy looked almost forlorn. Which made no sense since Morgan wasn't a rancher. All the Farradays came from ranching stock, but the next generation in Oklahoma had simply found branching out into construction more lucrative.

"There are so many things that are just about West Texas." Valerie paused while Ruth Ann dealt her into the game. "I freely admit I love these jeans and cowboy boots, but I don't understand how nobody misses shopping centers, movie theaters, live performances, and fine dining. Not that I get to do most of those very often, but at least having the option once in a while is nice."

"Well, there is Butler Springs," Dorothy suggested even though everyone at the table knew that didn't come close to the kind of entertainment and shopping Valerie meant.

Holding her cards against her chest, Valerie shivered momentarily. "Then there are the snakes. They're ugly, scary, and from what I understand, everywhere, not just out at the ghost town."

"She does have a point. It is West Texas." Donna appeared beside Valerie with a pitcher of tea. If she'd been any closer Eileen would've kicked her.

"I suppose the California girl in me might be overreacting to the guns, and the cows, and the horses and how everyone seems to know how to handle all three of those before kindergarten. Well, maybe not the gun part, but I saw all of Stacey's ribbons from the rodeo. No," she shook her head, "I'd have made a lousy rancher. I'm a So-Cal girl through and through."

There wasn't much Eileen could do about the shopping, the theater, the horses, and the cows, but there was one thing she might be able to fix. "When will your work be taking you back to California?"

"There's really no reason to stay. I should be heading back some time tomorrow."

Tomorrow. With a little help, that would give her just enough time. Who said West Texas couldn't do fine dining?

"Thank you. I'll shoot you an email later today." Morgan disconnected the call and closed the cover on the key lock box. This morning he'd woken up feeling unsettled. Out of sorts. He knew the reason why, but he refused to admit it to himself. He and Valerie had danced most of the night. She'd fallen in love with the two step and took every opportunity to participate any time a suitable tune came on. He, on the other hand, had taken it upon himself to make sure all those opportunities had been with him. When he got home, he really did need to thank his mother for insisting on all those dance lessons.

He didn't know what time tomorrow Valerie was

leaving town, but he knew he wanted to see her again before she left. Too bad the pub was closed on Monday nights; he would relish another chance to have at least one more dance with her.

On the sidewalk of the same street as Adam and Meg's home, he turned up the block to their house, surprised and delighted to see Valerie coming down the front steps. "Hello."

"Well, this is a nice surprise." The genuine delight on her face made him stand a little straighter.

"I was just coming to see you."

"That's a coincidence. Toni mentioned you were having lunch at the café."

"Just finished not long ago. Had some business to take care of in town." About to toe at the dirt along the sidewalks edge, he stopped himself from fidgeting like a nervous teen. "I know this is your last night in town."

She nodded.

"Butler Springs isn't too long a drive, but if you're up to it, I'd love to take you for that delicious steak dinner at the restaurant my brother raved about." Filtered in with Neil's other casual efforts at flirtation, the mention of the only steakhouse within driving distance was the only good thing Morgan gleaned from the entire interaction.

"Oh, I can't."

He nodded and took a step back. Shame on him.

"You don't understand." She reached for his arm. "I promised Jaime and Abbie that I would do a test run at the pub."

"Test run for what?"

"A fine dining experience. That's why I was heading to the café. I wanted to ask you in person if you'd be available to join me."

A wave of relief lifted his spirits and brought a smile to his face. "At least we both appear to have had the same basic idea. I'd be delighted to help Jaime out."

She slapped her hands together contentedly. "Terrific."

"Though, this is the first I've heard of new plans for dining at the pub. Wonder why he didn't come to the family?"

"According to Abbie, Jamie wants the critical opinion of an out of towner. Or as you have so often mentioned, a city girl."

"That does make sense. Most folks around here think Frank's meatloaf constitutes fine dining." He lifted his hands palms out. "Not that I don't want Frank's meatloaf, it's actually seriously delicious, but—"

"I get it. There's a lot to be said for comfort food, but it is an entirely different experience."

"What time shall I pick you up?"

Valerie looked at her wrist. "I know you have to get back to the ranch at a reasonable hour tonight. How about six?"

"Six is fine. And I promise, no matter the time, I won't turn into a pumpkin."

The entire ride back to the ranch, Morgan kept wondering why Jamie would want to open a fine dining establishment when the pub already did such a booming business over the weekends. It made no sense, but who was he to question his cousin. The guy ran a successful operation. So what if he wanted to expand.

"Well, you've certainly got a spring in your step." His aunt smiled up at him from the kitchen sink.

There was no arguing that his mood this afternoon was a vast improvement compared to when he'd woken up. The credit for his mood change fell squarely on Valerie Moore's shoulders. The woman was pretty special, and if he didn't watch his step he was going to fall head over boots in love with her. Heaven knew he was already more than halfway... there. The unexpected thought tripped in his mind.

"I didn't bring a dinner jacket. Do you think Uncle Sean would mind if I borrowed something of his?"

"I don't think he'd mind at all. Where do you need a dinner jacket in these parts?"

"Jamie is testing out some special menu tonight so I figured if he was going to the trouble of upscaling his business, the least I could do is wear a dinner jacket." For Jamie and Valerie. She'd done so much to fit into his world, the least he could do was wear a jacket to fit into hers. It was a good thing on occasions like this that the Farraday men were all cut from the same cloth. With a few exceptions, they were pretty much all the same height and size.

"Sounds good to me." One of the two cattle dogs came and scratched at the back door. Aunt Eileen let the pups in and turned back around to face Morgan. "Go ahead and look in his closet." She waved her thumb over her shoulder in the direction of their bedroom. "Help yourself to anything you like."

Gray, the larger of the two cattle dogs, stopped at his feet, dropped to his haunches and Morgan would have testified in a court of law that the animal smiled at him. Gently, he scratched the top of the dog's head for a minute before walking away. A few steps down the hall to the bedroom, he could've sworn he heard his aunt telling the dog he was right. The funnier thing, he was pretty positive he heard her apologize to the dog for ever doubting him. Maybe she was spending a little too much time alone in the ranch house. He was going to have to talk to his uncle about it the first chance he got.

A shower, a shave, and his favorite pressed shirt later, Morgan was back out the front door. Silently he said a small prayer his aunt wouldn't notice that he'd picked a few blooms from her front garden. Normally he'd stop at a flower shop, but there was no time today. The bright smile on Val's face when he presented her with the bouquet proved once again that a simple heartfelt gesture could win over any girl's heart.

His own words gave him pause. Was that what he was trying to do? Win her heart? He really needed to get a grip.

"Come in a minute while I get a vase from Meg."

"Take your time." His gaze lingered on her back walking away, but his mind was stuck on the vision of classic beauty a moment before. The woman had on a simple black dress that hugged just the right amount at every curve without looking clingy and cheap. Her hair was swirled up at the back of her head, drawing his eye to that deliciously long neck and a strand of simple pearls that draped perfectly between, well, draped perfectly. He needed to get his head on straight. This was a casual dinner date among friends, and it would do him good to remember that.

A few minutes later he'd said his howdee dos to his cousin and ushered Valerie out the door, around the corner, and under the quiet of the large oak trees. The walk to the pub was a short one. Everything in Tuckers Bluff was a short walk.

"I really appreciate you're coming with me. I'd feel a little too much like a food critic sitting at a table all by myself."

"I'm glad you asked me." Despite his own little anti-pep talk only a few moments ago, he reached for her hand and felt the adrenaline rush of a teen on his first real date. He was going to hate letting go when they reached O'Fearadaigh's.

CHAPTER TWELVE

From the bottom of Meg's street, the pub came into view. They walked the remaining distance without saying another word. The odd thing was he didn't feel the need to fill the quiet with empty words. He'd always thought the terms comfortable silence made no sense. How could silence be comfortable? Turns out being perfectly happy with a person without saying a word was really a thing. A good thing.

At the door, Morgan pulled on the massive ornate brass handle and relinquishing her hand, waved her inside.

"Oh my."

The splattering of pub height tables were gone and the remaining tables were draped in white clothes. The soft glow of candlelight gave the space a warm feel. The contrast to the normally almost cave-like darkness of the Irish pub was almost unsettling. It took a moment to notice the soft melodic tunes playing overhead. Nothing like the Irish fare that normally filled the air of O'Fearadaigh's. Just inside the door, a podium sported a scripted sign, *Please wait to be seated*. Not that they had to wait very long.

"Welcome to Chez Farraday." In a dark green evening dress, Meg arrived at the podium. "We have reserved the best table in the house for you. If you'll follow me."

When Valerie had mentioned they wanted her to be guinea pig to a fine dining experience, he'd thought it meant the food, not the ambiance. To Morgan's surprise, once they were seated, Meg set aside the white linen napkin and instead whipped out a black one to spread across Val's lap as well as a black napkin for his dark pants.

"Your waitress this evening will be with you

momentarily. Enjoy your dinner."

Meg turned on her heel and Jamie appeared out of nowhere to fill their glasses with water. So startled by the whole conversion, he hadn't noticed the water goblets on the table along with two more goblets, one slightly larger than the other for their choice of wine.

Next to appear dressed in black slacks and a white shirt was Jamison Farraday's better half.

"Good evening. My name is Abigail and I will be your server this evening." Abbie proceeded to recite the evening's menu and specials.

So enthralled with the entire production, Morgan hadn't really heard another word she'd said.

"It all sounds so wonderful." Valerie smiled up at Abbie. "I'd like to start with the champagne brie soup, then the goat cheese salad sounds delicious, and the grilled sea bass. And a pinot grigio please."

"Very well. And you, sir?"

Since he didn't have the heart to make her repeat her opening spiel, Morgan opted for the easy way out. "I'll have what the lady is having." Though now that he thought about it, the goat cheese salad wasn't likely to be his thing, but the company was what really mattered.

"I'll have your wine coming right out." Abbie pivoted and paused briefly at the bar before proceeding to the kitchen.

"I'm flabbergasted." Valerie took a sip of her water.

Morgan nodded. "It looks very different."

"Feels different. I mean, if I look closely I can tell it was the pub, but just sitting here the ambiance is completely and totally different. Nice."

Abbie re-appeared with their wines and a silver basket of warm bread. "The soup will be out momentarily. Can I get you anything else in the meantime?"

"No, thank you." Val looked around again. "You guys did an amazing job. If the food is even half as good, I know it will be fantastic."

"Thank you, I'd better go check on Frank. He was a little nervous about all this."

"Frank?" Morgan's voice dropped. "As in café cook Frank?"

"That would be the one." Abbie laughed. "Apparently he's about more than meatloaf and pot roast. If you'll excuse me."

Valerie reached for the bread and waited until Abbie was out of earshot. "I'm not sure if I should be highly intrigued, or absolutely terrified."

"I'm leaning towards intrigue, but I admit I would be less worried if the menu called for French onion soup. But how badly can someone ruin champagne, or cheese?"

Fingers splayed against her chest, Valerie both frowned and smiled, shaking her head. "I really do wish you hadn't asked that question."

"Sorry." He smiled and almost swallowed his tongue at the low moan that escaped from deep in Valerie's throat as she broke open the warm roll.

"Oh, this reminds me of the Italian bread you buy at Arthur Avenue in the Bronx." She pulled off another small nibble and popping it into her mouth moaned again. "As an intern I got to work on a production filming in New York. LA has some great restaurants, don't get me wrong, but I've never forgotten the Italian bread in New York. This definitely tastes like Arthur Avenue."

"I'm sorry, Arthur Avenue?"

"Little Italy." She reached for the butter. "This is definitely good enough to eat on its own, but I can't resist a little bread with my butter."

He chuckled at her play on words and the massive amount of butter she'd slathered onto the small piece of bread. "My money is on Toni. She's a great baker, and she's from Boston. If anybody around here would have even the slightest inkling of how to bake Italian bread, it would have to be her."

"Now I really don't know what to expect with dinner."

He tipped his head toward the back hallway. "We'll find out soon enough. Here she comes."

Abigail set a large bowl in front of Valerie first, then Morgan. Next she turned to the tray behind her and held out a massive pepper grinder. "Would you like some pepper?"

"No, thank you." Valerie shook her head.

"Thank you, me neither."

Since Abbie didn't make any effort to move, Morgan figured she was waiting for their reaction.

Taking the soup spoon in hand, he dipped it half way, made every effort to scoop a little up without spilling, and then took his first sip. "Okay, this is delicious."

Abbie's tentative expression gave way to a huge grin. When she bobbed her head slightly at her husband behind the bar, Jamie's grin widened to match hers.

"Delicious is an understatement." Valerie dipped her spoon into the soup again. "I may have to place an order or ten to go."

Abbie barked a hearty cackle and stepped back. "I'll let Frank know." And with those brief words, she was gone.

"This is so good. I don't care how many calories there are. I can't believe a former Marine mess hall cook made this soup." Valerie blew on another spoonful.

"Apparently, Frank is full of surprises." Morgan didn't say another word until his bowl was empty. "I don't know about you, but I'm thinking five stars."

"Not enough." She finished off the last few spoonfuls, dabbed at either corner of her mouth with her napkin, then leaned back in her seat. "If I were to die this minute, I would die a happy woman."

Morgan chuckled. "There you go, a life fulfilled by soup. But I can't blame you. I feel the same way."

"You know the best part?" she asked.

"What?"

"I didn't have to cook any of it. And you know what else?"

He shook his head.

"This whole thing has so blown my mind. The absolute best service, ambiance, and so far food, in the middle of a one restaurant town. I wouldn't be surprised if the dishes and furniture were to come to life and start dancing around the room."

"Okay. I have to disagree. I would be shocked as hell if

my silverware began dancing on the table about now."

That made Valerie laugh even harder. "What I mean is, this whole meal is proving to be the perfect night. The perfect end to my stay."

He tried very hard to keep a straight face. There was nothing perfect about ending her stay and he knew it.

Valerie couldn't think of a nicer way to spend her last evening in Tuckers Bluff. She'd meant what she'd said. Everything was truly perfect. The food *and* the company, and not necessarily in that order. When the salad arrived, she'd been surprised to find the almond-crusted goat cheese was actually warm and not sprinkled atop.

"Wow." She tried not to moan with delight. "I thought the soup would be the highlight and this would just be a salad. I think I was wrong."

Morgan looked less than convinced as his fork prodded at the baby spinach and candied almonds surrounding the wafer of warm cheese.

"Try it. You'll see."

One brow rose high on his forehead as he glanced down and skewered a morsel of cheese. This time, he was the one to groan at the surprise burst of flavor. "Remind me never to doubt you again."

She chuckled and waved her fork at him. Not very well mannered for such a surprisingly swank supper, but she couldn't remember the last time she'd enjoyed dinner, or the company, so much. "Absolutely."

"I bet you will at that." His grin widened as he more eagerly stabbed at another mouthful.

"I can honestly say every forkful is heaven. So far dinner is two for two."

Morgan nodded. "Who knew salad could taste like this."

Somewhere between oohing and aahing over the soup and salad, Valerie had been slow to notice the music had shifted from soft instrumental, to smooth vocalist renditions. Right now someone was doing one hell of a job belting out *What a Difference a Day Makes.*

"Oh wow." Morgan looked up.

"Now it's my turn. What?"

"I'm pretty sure that's Aunt Eileen."

Val looked over her shoulder, expecting to see the woman walking up the hall or away from the bar. "Where?"

A single finger pointed straight up to the ceiling even though the speakers were nowhere near them. Pushing his chair away from the table, he extended his hand to her. "May I have this dance?"

Thinking, she bit down on her lower lip and considered all she was up against. What was one little dance going to hurt. "I'd love to, but you'll need to explain about your aunt."

He nodded and led her to the floor. Like she'd done the night before, she molded against him as if she'd been designed just for him. On the small area cleared for a dance floor, he spun her around and pulled her close again. "We always knew Aunt Eileen could sing beautifully. She'd sung to all of us most of our lives. Especially if we were feeling under the weather. At some point, we had learned Aunt Eileen had given up her fiancé to take care of her sister's brood."

Valerie nodded. She vaguely remembered that being mentioned briefly in conversation over the last week or so.

"Turns out the fiancé came with a singing career."

"You're kidding?" Not that she didn't believe it, but she sure hadn't expected to hear that.

"As in albums recorded and the whole shebang." He momentarily let go of her hand and pointed up again. "This is her."

Val paused to listen, really listen. "She's amazing."

"In more ways than one."

"This town and your family are full of surprises."

"Life is never boring." He pulled her hand in closer between them. "And if we can't keep you entertained, we'll find something. Whether it's moonshine bootleggers, or—"

"A ghost town?"

He nodded, his eyes twinkling with humor. "And from the way the town has been talking, a few ghosts to go with it."

"Did anyone find it interesting that the only room affected by the ghost was Ted's room?"

"Well, there was the sugar incident."

"True," she nodded, "but the moving furniture, the voices, the music—"

"Music? What was that?"

"Ted again. Heard music, thought someone had set an alarm, but there was no alarm clock in the room."

"I wonder if Ted drinks and no one knows it?"

"That's quite a leap."

"Shorter than ghosts. Or do you believe in ghosts?"

"Let's just say I try to keep an open mind."

"Fair enough." She laughed. "What's the story about moonshiners?"

"From what I've heard, Ian was involved in catching some bootleggers who were racing local moonshine across state line and using Tuckers Bluff as a base."

"And the town looks so sweet. Were they locals?"

He nodded. "Sort of. Believe it or not, the town temperance leader, Mabel Berkner, who fought harder than anyone to keep the town dry—the culprit was her nephew."

"Oh, that is straight out of a movie of the week."

"Rumor has it that the aunt was actually the ring leader."

"Good grief." Her head tipped back with laughter. "If I'm ever low on material I know where to come."

His warm smile slipped. "Will you? Come back?"

How she wished she knew. "If a pilot is ordered then we'll be back to film."

"And if it doesn't?"

She blew out a short sigh. "I suppose if I had a reason."

"For business?"

The overhead tune changed, their steps slowed, and the air between them had grown thick. Suddenly thinking seemed impossible, finding her voice even harder. "I don't know."

His head bobbed once, then his chin dipped and his breath warmed her clear to her toes an instant before his lips found hers. The touch was tender, sweet, soft, and all too brief. He pulled back and his eyes seemed to be reading straight to her soul.

A loudly clearing throat followed by a noisy clattering of dishes broke the connection. Abbie carefully kept her back to the couple and seemed to be taking great care to make as much noise as possible serving the meal.

Still holding tightly to her hand, Morgan took a step in retreat. "Dinner's getting cold."

Nothing felt right anymore. Not eating dinner, not leaving the dance floor, not letting go of his hand, and certainly not leaving town. How could her world suddenly feel so off kilter in such a short time?

CHAPTER THIRTEEN

Valerie did a quiet fist pump and spinning around, all but danced a jig in her office. "Yes. Glad you agree."

Marilyn waved a thumbs up at her. From the few words Valerie had said during the call, it was unlikely Marilyn knew why Val was so happy, but like any good friend she was ready to cheer her bestie on.

"Oh, but…" Val stopped pacing and stared out the large plate glass window. "I understand, but my intention…" Pinching the bridge of her nose, Val huffed out a deep breath and slid into the nearby chair. "I see. Yes. Will get on it right away."

"For a minute there I thought lunch might be upgraded from burgers and fries to steak and champagne, but the sudden slip in your expression makes me wonder if we just downgraded to soup and salad."

Looking down, she tossed her phone onto the desk and turned to Marilyn. "The network loved the sizzle reel. They thought the construction cousins had all the right looks and the right rapport, but they loved the city slicker playing Texan."

"I thought you said the construction cousins were all Texas cowboys?"

"Oklahoma, but from what I could see, it's all more or less the same thing."

"Somehow I don't think a Texan would agree with you on that, but who's the city slicker?"

"Apparently, I am."

"You?"

Val nodded. "I may have dressed the part a bit."

"That explains a lot."

"Explains what?"

"Why you wore jeans and boots out for drinks last week."

"They're comfortable."

"Yes, that's what you said then too. So you're the city slicker."

Sometimes Marilyn was a little slow to catch on, but eventually she did. Like right about now. Her eyes grew perfectly round under brows arched high on her forehead. Yep. She'd put two and two together.

"They want you to actually appear in your own shows?" Marilyn couldn't have looked more surprised if someone had told her God wanted her to build another ark.

"Maybe."

"Maybe?"

"They liked the comic relief. A foible for the three perfect siblings."

"So they want you to be the quirky character that makes every new show a hit?"

Val thought of herself in many lights. After all, no real person was only two dimensional, but quirky wasn't one of the lights she considered her own.

"Do I get to see what it was you did that was so appealing?"

"The production company shot the network the sizzle reel and a cut scenes reel."

Marilyn chuckled. "In case they didn't love the good stuff, save it with bloopers."

"Not necessarily, but, you know how it is. Sometimes they turn out to be as important to a series success as the show itself."

"So now what?"

For weeks, she'd been asking herself the same question. Everything she did gave her reason to think. Shopping with Marilyn she found herself looking at designer boots and wondering if they could possibly be as comfortable as the ones Toni had given her. Dinner with her CPA at what used to be her favorite upscale restaurant didn't seem so favorite anymore. Dolling up for the premiere of a film her friend had edited seemed more like work than fun. Relaxing on the beach alone Sunday afternoon felt more alone than relaxing. Instead the chaos of the large gathering of Farradays for a ritual after church meal seemed more restorative than chaotic. And she missed it—*him.*

She was going back. This time she'd have a bigger budget and a full team to go with it. Production Manager, Line Producer. She'd been putting the pieces together, hoping her gut was right and the network would greenlight the pilot. After that, the series. Then she'd have a reason to stay longer. All she had to do was convince him to do the same.

Five fingers waved in front of her face. "Earth to Valerie."

"Hm?"

"I asked now what?"

"Oh, sorry. I was coordinating in my head."

"For the show?"

Among other things. "Yes. I'll be leaving Monday."

"That fast?"

A smile pulled at the corner of her mouth. "I've been ready for weeks." Heck, a couple of times, she'd come within inches of booking a flight and heading back, only to remind herself that her world was here. Then again, suddenly she wasn't so sure where her world was, and since she was all set to pull the trigger on this anyhow, what harm would it do to leave a little sooner?

"I'll mash the potatoes." Finn pulled a hand-held masher from the drawer.

"Don't skimp on the butter." Aunt Eileen slid a sheet of biscuits into the oven.

"No, Ma'am," Finn answered quickly.

Standing by the silverware drawer, Joanna counted out the forks. "Are we expecting anyone else or is this it?"

"Meg and Adam are coming straight from the airport." Aunt Eileen retrieved a pitcher of tea from the fridge.

"Airport?" Morgan wiped his feet at the back door. "Allison called away again?"

"Not me." Ethan's wife came in from the dining room and placed the extra napkins back in the pantry. "I'm staying put for a while."

"Meg and Adam offered to pick Valerie up at the Midland airport." Joanna carried a fist full of silverware to the dining room.

At the sink, Catherine rinsed out a sippy cup. "That was nice of them."

"Seemed the neighborly thing to do seeing as her project has drawn so much attention." Sean Farraday kissed his wife on the cheek. "Fiona has eaten all of Caitlin's Cheerios. Do we have any more?"

Aunt Eileen nodded. "In the pantry on the left. There's a stack of small pre-filled containers. Take as many as you need."

"Got it." Sean smiled, gave his wife's rear a gentle pat, and crossed the kitchen.

"You checking on your horse?" Eileen glanced over her shoulder at Morgan.

He nodded. "Looks good. The stumble earlier today doesn't seem to have caused any damage. Nothing's swollen or heated, but I'll check on her again later before I go home. Just to be sure."

"Good thinking. Better safe than sorry." Aunt Eileen leaned into Finn, looking at the contents of the pot.

"How's the project coming?" Finn spoke to Morgan as he handed a forkful of mashed potato to his aunt for her approval.

"Good." Morgan loved how the family interacted. There were the occasional squabbles and disagreements. The wilting glares from his aunt when she clearly disapproved of someone's choices. But for the most part Sunday supper was all about connecting. Not everyone made it every week, but most did, some more than others. And of course, everyone pitched in their share. Maybe if any of his brothers were married their house would be the same, but he doubted it. He loved his mother, but she'd always been more of a do-it-herself kind of mom when it came to the kitchen. He pilfered a cherry tomato from the salad Becky was tossing together. "Moving along faster than I expected."

"Faster is usually a good thing." Finn smiled at his aunt's nod of approval and covered the pot. "Isn't it?"

"Yeah. If nothing else I'll come in under budget when it comes to interest. Every penny saved helps."

"At least interest rates aren't what they used to be." Ryan came into the kitchen and pulled open the fridge door. "Are we out of tea?"

"It's already on the dining room table." Aunt Eileen pointed to the other room.

Empty glass in hand, Ryan nodded and spun about. From the living room a sudden burst of extra chatter sounded.

"And there they are." Aunt Eileen wiped her hands on a nearby dishrag and hurried out to meet her guest.

As soon as the grapevine in Tuckers Bluff spread the news of the impending pilot to be filmed, Morgan had been anxiously awaiting Valerie's arrival. Working with headphones on, he'd missed her call the other day and they had played telephone tag ever since. He had to hear the update from his brother Neil. With at least two of his brothers on board to do the pilot, he'd agreed to participate for completely different reasons. Not that he didn't agree with Quinn's reasoning. Most of the brothers were of the mind that if the show were to become a hit, it would be a boom for the family business in Oklahoma. Everybody and their uncle would want to use the construction cousins for their project. Heck, there'd even been a moment of joking around to change the name of the family business to Construction Cousins, but his interest rested more with a certain blonde city girl coming through the front door.

In complete contrast to the fashionable woman he'd first laid eyes on in the back hall of Abbie's café, his gaze landed on a casually dressed blonde. Her hair flipping about in a ponytail, her sleeves rolled up her forearm as though ready to take on a day's work, and her boots had that newly store-bought shine to them—but nothing a day on West Texas dirt wouldn't fix—and of course her favorite blingy sunshades rested on her head. But it was the Stetson still in her hand that really made him smile. He'd learned early on the hats were more for the sun than the fashion, but she must have been a sight getting on an airplane in sunny Southern California dressed like a true Texan. Nothing about the way she moved around greeting all the adults and cooing with the little ones, resembled a person out of their element trying to fit in. His city girl looked every bit the part of a country woman.

Listen to him. *His* city girl. As if a couple of evenings dancing and solitary toe tingling kiss gave him the right to call her his anything. But there was no denying, that's how he felt. The question remaining was what the heck was he going to do about it.

The crowd gathered in the front hall thinned and her gaze lifted, meeting his. He'd give anything to know what was going on behind those big blue eyes. An already sweet smile widened and pierced him with a burst of Neanderthal pride. His chest filled and his shoulders straightened, knowing that huge grin that made her eyes twinkle was meant for him. Just him.

"Okay." Aunt Eileen clapped her hands. "Dinner's getting cold."

It took a few minutes of shuffling around and a little careful maneuvering on his part to make sure he got to sit beside Valerie. Next, bowls of food were passed about and the din of chatter filled the room, occasionally spiking with a dispersed squeal from one young toddler or another. All in all, Morgan loved it.

"Sounds like the plans are all in place." Sean reached for a second helping of creamed corn.

Valerie nodded. "I've been working on setting things up since I left."

"You were that sure?" Morgan asked.

She stabbed at the last bite of beef on her dish. "Yep. I've known since the first tickling of the idea that this was going to fly high. Especially with the network looking for another reality show from me. It was pretty much a slam dunk."

"Well, at least we're glad to have you back."

"At least?" Valerie looked to Aunt Eileen.

"There's been a bit of chatter since you left." Aunt Eileen set her napkin on the table. "You know how fish stories grow. Seems the same thing happens with ghost stories."

Val blew out a short breath. "Yeah, the cameraman was so spooked that he refused to work on this project. I almost lost the whole production company."

"I'm afraid the sisters are spooked again." Sean pushed away from the table and picked up his empty plates. "You might want to take some extra measures to reassure them."

"Since the only room to have issues was Ted's room, I've already decided that I'm going to stay in that room. I don't care if the furniture levitates or Lady Macbeth pops up stirring her cauldron, I'll keep my mouth shut."

Most of the family laughed at her stab at ghostly apparitions. Even though Morgan didn't believe in ghosts, his gut still wanted him to stand sentry at her door, or better yet, park himself all night in her room. Not the best idea he'd ever had.

"Who's up for dessert?" Aunt Eileen stood up. "There's blueberry sour cream and cinnamon apple crumb cake."

A choir of voices called out for one or the other as people shifted around, clearing the table and carrying things to the kitchen. The perfect time for Morgan to escape a few minutes and check the barn. "If you'll excuse me a minute, I'll be right back."

"Checking on the horse again?" Aunt Eileen asked from the doorway.

Morgan nodded.

"Oh," Valerie stood, "may I come too?"

Morgan's head snapped around. Was this the same woman who shook merely standing in the same barn with Cinnamon?

"Good idea." Aunt Eileen didn't wait for Morgan to

respond. "You can make sure he doesn't miss dessert sitting with his horse."

"Will do," Valerie agreed.

Just like the night they'd walked to the pub for dinner, the walk to the barn was made in that same comfortable silence.

This time, instead of standing back and watching him, Valerie walked up to the stall where Cinnamon's head hung into the hallway, and reaching up, she scratched down the horse's nose. "Aren't you looking sweet."

Morgan had to blink. For a long minute he thought his eyes were fooling him.

"Did you bring any carrots?" she asked.

"Hang on." He took a minute to grab some treats from the tack room. "She should like one of these."

Before he could tell her how to feed the mare, the treat was on her open palm, the horse was gathering it up, and Val was giggling at the sensations.

"I'm sorry, but weren't you afraid of horses. No, wait. Terrified?"

She rolled her shoulders in a casual shrug. "Everyone fears what they don't know."

"And now you know horses?"

"Texas is a different world from California. We think we know that, understand that, almost expect that few places are like California, but until you spend time here it doesn't quite sink in." She went back to petting Cinnamon's nose. "Guns, cows, and horses are as much a part of this world as rattle snakes, hot summers, and friendly neighbors.

"There isn't much a girl can do in California about guns. I could probably have found a rancher in central California willing to teach me about cows, but it seemed easier and more practical to learn about horses. Surprisingly for me, the LA area is full of equestrian options. Who knew LA has a plethora of great trails for riding. I've made my way through the foothills and along the shore. Maybe some day I'll add West Texas to my list." Her gaze locked on his. "You know, and feel like those pioneers must have felt a million years ago. Riding with nothing in the way but grass blowing in the wind and the horizon."

He couldn't hold back a grin at her reference to their conversation that first day in Three Corners. Even though she made it sound casual as heck, it must have taken a lot for her to lose the paralyzing fear she'd displayed not so very long ago. And for what? To better understand his world. Nothing complicated about that. Which made him wonder, what other surprises did his new country girl have in store for him?

CHAPTER FOURTEEN

S o far so good. They'd settled into the brothel last night and Valerie realized she'd won the bedroom lottery. From what she could gather from the few pieces that the sisters told her were original to the room, and now knowing this was the largest room in the establishment, she guessed this must have been the infamous Miss Sadie's boudoir.

That word made her smile. The sisters had done a fabulous job of keeping the original feel of the era with an air of modern comforts. The mattress was probably one of the best she'd ever slept on, including her own. She had no idea what Ted had been talking about. She had the best night sleep she'd had in a long time and every single piece of furniture was in exactly the same place this morning that it had been in last night. Except for the dish and that didn't count as furniture.

"I'm sorry," the cameraman from the sizzle shoot who hadn't been scared off by imaginary ghosts came up to her. "I'm sorry Val, but I just can't get in close enough without getting in the way for some of these shots you want."

"I was afraid of that." One of the things she'd noticed when they'd done the sizzle reel were the expressions the brothers made while working. Though the brothers all had that Farraday look to them, the only time they actually looked almost identical was when they made certain faces, and those faces were specifically related to some working task. She felt if the camera zoomed in and out on the brothers making that same face, the surprise factor could be popular with an audience. She really wanted it. "Got any suggestions?"

"Actually, what if we use the Go Pro?"

That could work. The tiny camera used mostly for outdoor sports and underwater image taking had been used before on sets. "What would we attach it to? Robot?"

The cameraman shook his head. "Didn't think we'd need one, so we didn't bring anything that small."

"So it's a no go?" Which had her wondering why did he bring it up at all.

"Actually." He waved a finger over his shoulder at a rather adorably ugly dog sniffing around the lunch spread. "We could strap it to her head. Edits can get the few seconds we need."

Val squatted on her haunches and the dog waddled over. "French bulldog, right?"

"That's my guess."

"Is she well trained?"

"Not very, but I bet if we just do a trail of hot dogs or dab the guys' faces with hot dog juice, our roving cameraman will get the shot."

"Sounds like a plan." She scratched the dog one quick minute behind its ears and pushed to her feet. "We'll give it a go."

According to her watch and her growling stomach, it was just about time for a lunch break. She was really pleased with how the morning had gone. Things couldn't have been better had the entire show been totally scripted. Well, except for when one of the production people flushed the toilet without ever turning off their microphone. But that won't be the first or last time it happens.

Standing off to one side, she watched the cameramen bait the dog. What an odd breed for a guy like that. She'd have pictured him owning something larger, like a golden retriever or a lab. Maybe even a mutt, but not something as prissy and popular as a French bulldog. Regardless, the effort came off without a hitch. The dog followed the trail right up to Neil's face and moments later did it again to Ryan. Yep. The production Gods were watching over her.

"Chow line is forming." Morgan sidled up beside her. "Planning on a bite to eat?"

"A bite? I was thinking an entire side of beef."

"This *is* cattle country."

"Oh," she cringed, "I wish you hadn't said it quite that way. I like thinking my steaks come from little cellophane packets at the grocery store with no previous links to the food chain."

Morgan threw his head back and barked out a laugh. He really did have a nice laugh. Nice smile, too. Who was she kidding? The man had a nice everything.

Anyone looking at the amount of food piled onto her plate would have thought she'd just been rescued from a deserted island.

"Hungry?" the same cameraman, Jim, snickered and bit into the biggest spare rib she'd ever seen.

Sliding onto the picnic table bench across from him, she rolled her eyes. "Just a little."

"Hey, a healthy appetite is good for ghostbusting." Apparently, Jim thought he had a sense of humor. "Speaking of which, how did you sleep last night?"

"Like a baby."

"Is that good or bad?"

"Great actually."

"So nothing went bang in the night?"

"Not even bump."

Morgan slid in beside her. "All is well with the haunted room?"

"Shh." She looked over her shoulder. "Don't even tease about that or I'll have half the crew and meal company running for the hills."

"Nah." Jim shrugged. "Most of us are made of stronger stuff."

"At least you didn't have any unexplained happenings." Morgan spread butter on his roll.

"Nothing like what happened to Ted, but I did get a visitor."

Morgan's eyes circled round. "Who?"

"Not exactly a who. More of a what."

"What?" Morgan and Jim echoed.

"I took some crackers to bed last night to nibble on as I went over the sheets for this morning."

"Okay." Morgan set his fork down. "And?"

"This morning when I woke up the wrapper was on the floor and most of the crackers were gone, some were just left in crumbs."

"Mice?" Morgan asked.

"I sure hope it isn't rats. Mice are bad enough." She spread her paper napkin across her lap. "I'm betting that the mouse, or mice, is what tripped someone's alarm clock that spooked Ted."

"What about the furniture?" Jim looked up. "Must have been one helluva mouse."

Morgan tried not to laugh. "He has a point. My money is still on Ted's a closet drinker."

"Nah." Jim shook his head. "I'm going with heavy sleeper with crazy dreams and possible sleepwalker."

"Whatever. At least that problem is over. Which reminds me," Valerie reached for a chip, "I really appreciate letting us use your dog to solve the camera problem."

"My dog?"

Valerie nodded.

"He's not mine." Jim shook his head. "I thought she was yours until you asked me if she was trained."

"Well, she must belong to someone." After all, dogs didn't just appear out of nowhere.

It was one thing getting used to knowing a camera was following your every move, it was another to have the big eared mutt in his face all the time. "Have we figured out who her owner is?"

"His." One of the cameramen, whose name Morgan didn't know yet, corrected him.

"His?" Morgan could have sworn Jim and Valerie had said that this morning's dog was a she. "Okay, whatever it is, any chance we skip the hot dog induced scenes for a while? I'm going to waste a lot of wood if *he* keeps trying to lick my face."

"Sure." The cameraman shrugged.

"Great. I'm going to go wash up a minute and I'll be right back. In the meantime, somebody find out who his owner is."

Hot dogs fresh from the grill with a little relish and mustard on a warm bun was a great midsummer treat, but rubbed on a person's face, even just a little, was miserable. This was definitely not what he'd signed up for.

"My, don't you look handsome this morning." The tall redheaded sister smiled proudly at him as though he were her own son.

"Yes, he does, doesn't he?" The shorter sister with the tall blonde hairstyle that had gone out of fashion long before he was born, beamed at him. Clearly, she had an olfactory issue. "I can't tell you how pleased we are to hear that Valerie didn't run into any issues last night. We were fretfully worried about her."

"That's right." The redhead nodded. "Hardly slept a wink."

From anyone else he would have thought the words were nothing more than lip service, but from the concerned expressions, Morgan was pretty sure they'd meant every word. "Now you can sleep easy tonight."

"Yes, yes we can." The blonde nodded.

"Speaking of Valerie, do either of you know where she is?" He needed a small mood booster and that pretty smile would be just the prescription.

"She was going to her room. Said she'd forgotten some notes." The blonde pointed up the stairs.

"Got it. Thanks ladies." He'd go wash off the scent of hot dogs and then casually loiter until Valerie came back.

The notes had to be here. Valerie crossed the room to the stack of receipts and miscellaneous toiletry items on the tall boy dresser, but still none of her shooting notes. She glanced at the floor and the nightstand and still nothing. Unless… squatting down on all fours it occurred to her that maybe it has slipped off the table and glided under the bed. She just hoped Mr. or Mrs. Mouse wasn't visiting under her bed.

Leaning a little sideways, she hunched over and the sight of two round green orbs had her falling back on her butt. Scooting quickly to one side, she got a grip of herself. After all, not even rats had eyes that large. Or green. Slowly easing back down the floor, she managed to get a better look. "Oh, for the love of Pete." She scooted down a little lower. "Here kitty, kitty. Come here." She tapped her fingers on the floor and when the cat didn't budge she tried drumming them on the old wood floor. Sitting up, Val wondered what the heck the cat was up to.

"Wouldn't you like a cracker?" Val still had an entire package in the box. Quickly grabbing one, she shoved it under the bed. If she'd learned anything about cats through the years, she was now completely convinced the animal snubbed her nose at Val. "I guess not."

Two seconds later, the cat broke the staring game and scurried low to the ground from one end of the bed to the other and dramatically, almost desperately, scratched at a crack in the baseboard. "Are you trying to tell me that's where our friend Mr. Mouse has gone?" Well, she had no intention of crawling under the bed after the cat or the mouse. Giving the bed a good shove, she managed to move it out of the way for a better line of sight of the cracked baseboard. Except it was too even for a crack. Tracing her finger along what she now realized was a seam, she pushed up on one foot, then the other, until she was nearly upright, feeling up the wall.

This was ridiculous. Now both she and the cat were on hind legs, arms against the wall, in search of what? A mouse? "This is silly." She looked down to tell the cat, leaned a little harder on the paneling board and the next thing she knew she'd fallen face forward, onto all fours, in a dark hole. "What the heck?"

She was either sitting in the strangest damn closet she'd ever seen, or she simply couldn't see into the black hole that she suspected went way deeper than where she sat. Scrambling onto all fours, she crawled back onto the bedroom carpet and checked the nightstand drawer. She had a vague recollection of seeing a flashlight in there. A tad unsteady on her feet, she reached for the nightstand and sure enough, one LED flashlight at her disposal. Thank heavens for modern technology.

"Okay." Val pushed the button, lighting up the long narrow corridor on the other side of the hidden door. "Ready for an adventure, Kitty?"

Pointing to the ceiling, the light bounced around the dark hole, illuminating the entire tunnel, not just the floor. A threat of fear, or maybe panic, clawed at her throat as she forced herself to put one foot in front of the other. Wasn't this the sort of thing horror movies were made of? Dumb blondes walking into the darkness rather than run to the big strong hero just outside. Well, even if it was, it was too late now. She'd committed herself to inch along the downward sloping tunnel.

What felt like a mile later—probably only because of the minced steps she was forced to take out of fear of falling and breaking her neck and never being found again—she reached a wall. A dead end much like the other walls that lined the tunnel. All she had to find was the lever. Somewhere.

Feeling blindly along the sides as she'd done in her room, she felt something click under her foot, and like Ali Baba's cave, the door swung open. Where the heck was she? One step inside, she waved the light forward and the beam bounced off the pews. The church. She was in the church. Now wasn't that an odd connection. The brothel Madame's bedroom and the church. Morgan wasn't kidding, this part of the country really did go out of their way to entertain—

A cold clammy hand clamped around her mouth, robbing her of words and thoughts and sending her heartbeat racing like a thoroughbred at the Kentucky Derby.

"Do not move," the deep raspy voice growled at her.

Damned if she wasn't one of those dumb blonde heroines too stupid to live after all.

CHAPTER FIFTEEN

"Knock knock," Morgan called as he rapped lightly on Valerie's door. His ear to the solid wooden surface, he called her name a little louder. One more knock and he slowly turned the knob, praying she wouldn't be mad as a hornet for this invasion of her privacy. The room was empty. No sign of her. How had he missed her? He hadn't closed the bathroom door when he'd washed his hands and he'd kept his eyes on the mirror in case she walked past him. Maybe when he'd turned to dry his hands?

A few more minutes without her smile wasn't going to kill him. This time trotting back to the construction spot, he scanned the surroundings for any sign of Valerie. Nothing. The hairs on the back of his neck were beginning to prickle. Nothing bad could happen out here in the happiest place in West Texas. Nothing really bad ever happened in Farraday country.

"You coming back to work or planning on catching rays the rest of the day?" Neil shouted up at him, no humor in his voice.

"Have you seen Valerie?"

Both brothers shook their heads.

"I'm sure she'll be back any minute," Jim offered, pulling back from filming Ryan.

The little dog was once again underfoot. "I thought someone was going to find his owner?"

"Her." Jim set the camera down and scooped the dog up into his arms. "I've asked everyone here. No one brought a dog."

Morgan might not be an animal expert, but he knew the

difference between a male and female dog. "Something's not right here. The dog that was all over me a short while ago was beyond any doubt a male."

Jim raised his brows and turned the pup in his arms belly up, shaking his head at the clearly female anatomy.

Not wanting to argue, Morgan put his fingers between his lips and blew loud and strong. From under the tablecloth by the food area another identical big eared dog came prancing over to him.

"There are two of them." Jim wasn't asking.

Neil walked over. "They don't look like they've been going hungry."

"This is awfully far for a couple of fancy dogs like that to be strolling around without their owners." Ryan looked up and down the street. "Hmm."

"What do you mean, hmm?" Morgan glanced up the street. Sitting, ears up, eyes piercing, a dog that looked a helluva lot like Grey was perched in front of the churchyard, staring him down. "I don't like this."

"Wonder what he's doing so far from home?" Neil took a step further into the street. "Think he hitched a ride in the back of a truck?"

Morgan didn't have time to process or respond when the other Farraday dog stepped out from behind the picket fence, and muzzle up, let out a sharp bark followed quickly by a short howl.

The two French bulldogs took off at a trot as if the dog had called them each by name.

"I really don't like this."

Ryan nodded. "Something feels off."

"And I can't find Valerie." Morgan didn't bother to wait for anyone else and tore off up the street after the pups. Not till he reached the edge of the churchyard did he realize his brothers were on his heels. All four dogs had run off between the church and hotel toward what had to be the back of the church. Raising his hand, he urged them to slow down as he carefully traced the dogs' footsteps and tried to figure this mess out.

Instincts told him to move slow and hug the wall. He

could hear a man's voice yelling.

"What the hell did you grab the girl for?"

The girl. Son of a… Morgan bit down hard on his back teeth.

"She saw us."

"You stupid idiot. All she could see is an empty church. If you'd have kept your lame brain hands to yourself she'd have left an empty church! Now we got to get rid of her. She's a witness."

Morgan's heart lurched to his throat. Witness to what?

"And what the hell are the dogs doing out here?"

"They looked lonesome all locked up in the kennel."

"Lonesome?" the first voice roared. "They're F-ing dogs. If anything happens to them, that's ten grand a piece down the tubes."

Morgan had inched his way close enough to see what was going on. A big beefy guy had Valerie in a near headlock, his hand over her mouth. One strong twist and he could easily snap her neck.

"Go ahead and get her in the car. Tie her up first and make sure she doesn't make a peep. There are enough television people crawling around here to cause us some serious trouble. Get her and these dogs out of sight."

Right about now he'd kill for his cousin DJ to come riding to the rescue. Morgan didn't have anything he could use for a weapon except the element of surprise. From where he stood it didn't look like either of the goons had a gun, but underestimating them could be deadly.

The beefy guy took a couple of steps backward and Valerie's legs flailed out from under her as her shorter legs tried to keep up.

When Morgan got his hands on the creep he was going to snap his neck in two. For now, he needed back up. Pulling out his phone he sent his brothers a text and hoped their phones were still on silent from filming.

NEED A DISTRACTING NOISE FROM BEHIND THE HOTEL AND ANOTHER FROM SOUTH OF THE CHURCH DIVIDE AND CONQUER. I'M GOING AFTER MR. BEEFY.

Two thumbs up emojis popped up on his phone, followed by

ON THE COUNT OF TEN. NOW.

His mind did the mental math, one, two, please God, five, six, make this work, nine and a bang sounded from his left and a clank from the right.

The skinny goon turned to rush south and the big guy seemed more confused than anything.

His arms straight in front of him, holding a screwdriver like a gun and hoping the sunlight would catch the steel just right, Morgan ran straight and fast and yelled as hard as he could. "Duck!"

Bless Valerie, she stomped down hard on her captor's arch, thrust an elbow in his gut and rolled away when the surprise of it all had Mr. Beefy letting go and scrambling to defend himself from Morgan in front and Ryan coming at him with a two by four from the side. All he could think was thank the lord Valerie was free.

It took Valerie several long minutes to catch her breath. More than once the buffoon who had grabbed her had nearly robbed her of all air. Lifting her head she was able to see the action ahead. Morgan had shoved the buffoon onto the ground, pummeling him with both fists. Either the idiot had a glass jaw, or Morgan was mad as hell.

"That's enough." Ryan dropped the piece of wood on the ground and was yanking his brother away from the guy who had almost strangled her.

His chest heaving with anger-fueled adrenaline, Morgan rolled back onto his heels and hurried to where Valerie sat holding her knees to her chest. "Are you okay? Did he hurt you?"

Her head shook from side to side. "Mostly scared me." From the look on his face the last thing she needed to tell them was that there had been a moment or two when she thought she'd never see him again.

The fear, the anguish, the adrenaline whooshed out of her like a deflated balloon the minute Morgan swooped her into his arms. She hated reacting like a little girl, but the tears gushed nonetheless. "I'm sorry."

His hold on her tightened ever so gently. "Don't be. You were magnificent."

That made her chuckle. "I don't know about that."

"Are you kidding me? You should have seen the look on his face when you stomped on him and then jabbed him. He never saw it coming."

"There wasn't a point sooner. I'd have never gotten far enough away to reach anyone, and with all the sawing and hammering I didn't think anyone would hear me scream."

By now, some of the cameramen had arrived. Neil and Jim had the skinny guy hog tied and Ryan stood over Mr. Beefy like a rodeo rider over a roped steer. The exception being that no one at the rodeo held a menacing two by four. "Looks like they've got this under control."

Valerie nodded, but didn't move.

"Oh my." Sister came running up. "Oh my, oh my."

A few feet behind her, Sissy kept shaking her head. "That's Mabel Berkner's nephew."

"Sure is," Sister confirmed.

"Didn't he and his mama Lily move far away?"

"Doesn't look like it, does it?" Sister shook her head.

Valerie figured the two sisters got it about right. Nowhere near far enough away.

Sirens blared in the background.

Neil came up to Morgan's side. "We texted DJ when we realized we might be out of our league. That should be him or Reed."

"Thanks." Morgan nodded at his brother but didn't let go of Valerie, and that was fine by her, except she couldn't very well stand here in his arms for the rest of the day.

She remained enfolded in Morgan's space until DJ pulled up behind the church.

"Well, look what we have here." DJ shook his head at

Mr. Beefy. "You really didn't learn your lesson, do you? Thought two years behind bars would have taught you to stay on the right side of the law. Want to tell me what this is all about?"

The nephew shook his head.

"You keep quiet," the skinny guy shouted. "A good lawyer will have us out in a couple of hours."

"Wasn't that what your buddy told you about running moonshine?" DJ spoke slow and steady as if any faster and Beefy might not understand.

"You keep your trap shut," the other guy yelled again as Reed slapped handcuffs on him and reading him his rights, shoved him into his patrol car.

"I'll meet you back at the station," DJ called to Reed. His deputy nodded and DJ waited till the dust had settled before turning back to Beefy. "Okay. Do you want to tell me what's going on now or do you want to tell the judge?"

"We were going to be richer than running moonshine," Beefy muttered.

"Go on," DJ urged.

Valerie stepped in closer. She didn't want to miss a word.

"It all started with some fancy parrot from Mexico. I could transport those wild critters in my car and no one could catch us." Beefy grinned. "Got paid better than moonshine too, but those stupid peacocks kept screeching at night. Can't hide from the law if the dumb birds don't shut up."

The sisters' ghosts were starting to make sense. Squawking peacocks really do sound a lot like women crying "help me."

"I'm still listening," DJ prompted.

"Turns out people pay a lot of money for those ugly bulldogs."

DJ followed Morgan's finger to where a couple of the crew held the wandering French bulldogs.

"So you've been stealing dogs and running them like you ran our moonshine." It wasn't a question.

Beefy nodded.

"And this place?"

Beefy shrugged. "Cheap rent and no nosy neighbors."

"What rent?" Sissy snapped, before mumbling she should send a bill to Mabel.

"One more question." Morgan looked to Beefy. "Why'd you move the furniture around?"

"Didn't want no movies being made here. People crawling around." He spit on the ground. "Look what happened." He pointed his chin at Valerie. "I was right. Messed everything up."

DJ turned to the folks standing around. "I'm going to need to get statements from everyone. When you have a minute, come on down to the station."

Heads bobbed, and Valerie slid out of Morgan's protection and walked up to the sisters. "Did you guys know there's a tunnel from my bedroom to the church?"

From the way both women's eyes rounded like a cartoon owl, she was pretty sure the answer was no. Guess she wasn't going to find out what the story was with Sadie and the church. Then again, maybe not all questions were meant to be answered.

CHAPTER SIXTEEN

Drinks in the air, the crowd gathering at O'Fearadaigh's to celebrate the wrap of the pilot chorused, *Sláinte*."

"Job well done." Aunt Eileen patted Morgan on the arm and he slid his hand atop hers.

"It's a good team." Sean Farraday raised his glass again.

"When will we know if they pick up the series?" Finn asked.

"Months." Val rolled her eyes skyward. "Editing alone will take about six weeks. There's a long list of steps, from clearing the rights to any music, sound effects, or stock footage and things, to the Rough Cut, Fine Cut, and Lock Cut. Then they'll go to Color and Mix to make sure everything is aesthetically pleasing and within legal broadcast standards. Yada yada yada."

"In other words, now we sit and wait," Neil said.

Valerie bobbed her head. "That about covers it."

"So," Jim looked to the fellows, "what do you guys do until then?"

Ryan laughed. "Depends who you ask. If you asked my mother there's the list as long as Valerie's for jobs to be done in Oklahoma. On the other hand, if you ask Aunt Eileen, there's a long list to be done right here in Tuckers Bluff."

"I'll be staying here for a little while longer." Under the table, Morgan squeezed Valerie's hand. "Or maybe it's time I took a vacation."

"I'm with big brother. The business almost runs itself some days. It won't miss the two of us." Neil fingered his glass of beer. "Oklahoma isn't nearly as exciting as Tuckers

Bluff."

His aunt smacked him gently on the arm. "Now don't you go making fun of us. A little variety in life is a good thing."

Neil held his hands palm out, fingers splayed. "Hey, I'm on your side. I'm liking the variety around here. If nothing else, it keeps us on our toes."

"You're just looking for another chance to hogtie something besides a calf." Ryan shook his head at his brother.

"You never know." Neil hefted a single shoulder.

"Atta boy," Hannah tipped her beer at her Oklahoma cousin. "Stick around and we'll show you how to have fun!"

Dale squeezed his wife's hand and with a smile muttered, "Always a firecracker."

Morgan flipped the O'Fearadaigh's cardboard coaster in his hand. "Tell me, Jamie, what did y'all decide about the fancy restaurant?"

Jamie cast a quick glance at his wife, who looked over to their aunt, who—no surprise—kept her gaze on her white wine. "I don't think the town is quite ready for upscale dining."

"But," Aunt Eileen looked to Valerie, "it's nice to know it could be done."

Smiling, Valerie seemed to get Aunt Eileen's message. Morgan wasn't sure all that work had been necessary. With every passing day, Val fit in more and more with the simple country life. Though she had thrown him for a loop when she showed off a brand spanking new pair of cowboy boots she had ordered online—in pink.

Uncle Sean drank down the last sip of his stout and pushed away from the table. "It's been a long day, and it's a long drive home. If y'all will excuse us." He held his hand out for Aunt Eileen and the two bid a quick goodbye to everyone, then walked out the door hand-in-hand.

"I still wonder what took those two so long to figure out they belonged together," Abbie mused.

Multiple voices at the table chorused *Amen*.

Abbie pushed her chair back and stood. "It's time I go get my son. It's almost his bath time, and that's pretty much his favorite activity of the day." She gave her husband a quick peck and hurried out the door.

One by one the family dispersed, heading to their own homes.

"So it looks like it's just the three Farraday cousins." Ryan tipped his glass at Valerie and smiled. "And company."

Neil bobbed his head. "Next round is on me."

"Sorry, fellows. It's been a long week, and I'm ready to crash," Valerie said.

Still holding her hand, Morgan pushed to his feet. "I'll walk you home."

"That'll be nice."

On purpose, Morgan didn't look at either of his brothers. He knew he'd be teased mercilessly when they all got back to the Farraday ranch, but he didn't care. Outside the pub, he tugged her a little closer as they walked.

"So you'll be staying here for a while?" she asked.

Morgan nodded. He'd been meaning to tell her about his project, but there never seemed to be a moment when something else wasn't happening. "At least six weeks. Maybe more."

"Is this that project y'all were talking about at dinner my first night back?"

He wondered if she'd heard herself say y'all instead of you guys. It sounded really pretty from her. "Yes, that's the one. Do you remember the house down the street from Meg?"

"The one with the missing library ladder?"

Somehow he knew that would be the part she'd most remember. The library. "Yep, that's the one. I bought it from the owner."

Her eyes popped open wide. "Really?"

"I knew whoever bought it at a bargain wasn't going to restore some of those old rooms. Especially not the library. With the growing popularity of ereaders and internet search engines, folks simply don't keep as many books around as they used to. Even public libraries are dying in some cities."

"I know. So sad."

"Anyhow, I thought if it were fully restored, maybe it would attract the right buyer. So, she and I came to an agreement. We settled on a fair price in the current condition, and for a small down payment, she's carrying the note."

"Oh. So you're planning on flipping it?"

That depended on so many things. "Maybe." He drew to a stop. "Want to come in and see?"

Her gaze darted about the front yard. He'd barely had time to do much more than attack the overgrowth but that alone had made a huge improvement to the curb appeal. "I'd love to."

Climbing the front steps to the wide veranda made Valerie almost giddy with delight. A person would think it was her house she was about to get a glimpse at.

Morgan drew the key from his pocket and turned the lock. The large wooden door with a typical glass window swung open.

"It's only primer."

"The ceilings look so much taller without the dirty walls."

"First thing I did was rewire the first floor, then scrape off the crud, sand and patch the rough spots."

"Wow. That's a lot. How long ago did you buy it?"

"The week you went back to California."

She nodded. So he'd had several weeks to work on it before she'd dragged him away again to film the pilot. "It really does look nice."

"It'll look even nicer with a fresh coat of paint. Something bright but not so institutional as solid white."

"Yeah. I think you're right."

Slowly, she perused different rooms on the first floor, and just like the first time they'd seen the house, the library was the last stop.

Morgan opened the double doors and stepped aside.

"Wow." She knew her mouth was hanging open but couldn't bring herself to snap it shut. Every inch of wood gleamed against the overhead lighting. "Just wow."

"It took quite a bit of sanding. There's three coats of polyurethane. This sucker should stay this beautiful for generations to come."

Slowly she ran her hand along the smooth, empty shelves. "This is magnificent." Standing in front of another shelf that held several books, she took a minute to read the spines. Biography of the Windsors, Paul Newman.

"I thought since you like romance and biography, you might want to borrow a book or two of some real life romances."

She quoted Paul Newman, "Why go out for hamburger when you have steak at home."

"Smart man." Morgan smiled.

Another shelf had mysteries and cozies and she wondered how did this man know her so well. Obviously she'd told him her taste, but he'd filed the data away to be retrieved when needed. She continued to circle the room while reading the sporadic spines of the occasional shelf of books when her arm bumped into the wall. Looking left, it wasn't a wall. A ladder. "I hate to keep repeating myself, but wow. I feel as though I've died and gone to book heaven."

Leaning against a wall of books, watching her, his arms and ankles crossed, he smiled.

And that's when she saw it. Almost the entire wall had been filled with books. The same wall she'd told him she'd want to fill with romances. Her heart did a flip and she eased forward. Almost afraid of what she might or might not find. "You remembered."

Only his head moved. "I remembered. All the wives helped."

She pulled out the first spine her fingers touched. "One of my favorite authors."

"So, you like?"

Holding the book close to her heart, she spun around to face him. "I love it."

Unfolding his arms, he stepped into her private space and tucked a loose lock of hair behind her ear. "I'd hoped you would."

She couldn't find any words, and could barely nod her head. The intensity of his gaze drilled through her all the way to her toes.

"If I were to say something stupid like I love you, would you turn and run?"

She shook her head and managed to mumble, "Not stupid."

"Good." He tucked the same strand of hair behind her ear again. "Because I love you."

His lips came down on hers with the same warmth and tenderness as the last time. For all the weeks they'd been apart waiting for the approval of the pilot, the memory of that one kiss had kept her heart light and her hopes high. When he gently eased back, her hand engulfed in each of his, she managed to move her lips. "I love you too."

"Does that mean we get to keep the library?"

Eyes closed, she didn't have a clue how to make that work, but she was sure of one thing. She desperately wanted to. Dipping her chin to her chest once, she leveled her gaze with his. "Abso-bloody-lutely."

EPILOGUE

"**W**hat time is it?" Valerie patted her pockets.

"If you're looking for your phone," seated in her favorite recliner, Aunt Eileen raised her arm up in the air and pointed her finger at a nearby table, "it's over here."

All through supper Valerie had been as fidgety as the proverbial long-tailed cat in a room full of rockers. Anyone would think she'd never produced a reality television show before in her life.

Morgan stretched his arm out, retrieved her phone, and patted the seat beside him. As soon as Valerie landed on the overstuffed sofa, she curled into his side and rested her head on his shoulder. "The show doesn't start for almost forty-five minutes. Believe me," Morgan reassured her with a kiss to the temple, "no one is going to let us forget the premiere."

"Someone remind me what name they settled on for the show?" Aunt Eileen scrolled through the on screen guide for live TV.

Val sank deeper into Morgan's side and called out, "Ghost Town Fixer."

"Oh, that's original." Aunt Eileen rolled her eyes.

The entire clan had descended on the Farraday house to watch the premier of the Construction Cousins fixing up a ghost town show on the new bigger screen, including most of the Oklahoma contingent. Well, except for their mom and dad. Neil still wished he had a hint of an idea what could have been so fracturing to keep the two branches of the same tree apart for so long.

From where he sat, he had a birds-eye view of just

about everyone. There was something about this place that seemed to promulgate loving happiness. Not a couple in the room seemed to have a care in the world. Not that he believed all the spouses got along with each other one hundred percent of the time, except maybe for Morgan and Valerie. Not a single minute that those two spent with Neil and rest of the brothers did either look anything but head over boot heels, wildly in love. If he could bottle all the energy zinging between one cousin or other and their wives, he'd be the wealthiest man alive.

"Oh, look!" Sitting on the loveseat with her husband, Grace pointed at the television commercial for tonight's first episode. "My, you are a rugged lot."

Morgan pointed at the TV, but looked at Valerie. "Have I mentioned you look great on horseback?"

Several voices in the room answered yes, rather strongly, moments before the room erupted with laughter.

Brooks leaned forward. "Who remembers painting Meg's B&B when Adam and she were dating?"

"Oh, good grief, don't remind us." DJ rolled his eyes.

Adam raised his brows at his younger brother. "Pot calling kettle black?"

There was no arguing that all the couples in the room, including Uncle Sean and Aunt Eileen, were truly and hopefully permanently besotted with each other. The word was old fashioned but somehow seemed to fit even in this modern world.

As Valerie leaned forward, Morgan's arm slid protectively from her shoulder to her waist. "Okay, here it comes."

The montage clip of all the brothers and some of the unexpected shenanigans came off sharp and entertaining. Neil nodded. "So far so good."

For the next thirty minutes they watched as the old emporium came back to life, from dusty worn shelves to the glossy clean look of fully stocked with all things local.

"That was really a brilliant idea." Aunt Eileen pushed to her feet. "Ken Brady was telling me that the weekend sales at the emporium of their wine outsell a month's worth at the winery."

"Sarah Sue has upped her jam production too." Becky followed the older woman into the kitchen. "Who knew there were so many tourists passing us by."

"Just needed a reason to stop." DJ slung his arm across his wife's shoulder.

One by one, and two by two, the family mulled about the kitchen until everyone was seated or hovering around the massive table and digging into their preferred dessert. It was Morgan and Valerie who held Neil's attention as he stabbed at a slice of Aunt Eileen's famed blueberry pie. The two hadn't budged from the sofa. He couldn't tell what they were saying to each other, but the intense way their gazes seemed almost unbreakably linked told him the subject matter was something more serious than pie or ice cream for dessert. The easy way Morgan's thumb caressed her hand had Neil almost mesmerized until Valerie's arms flew around his brother's neck and the sweet moment turned very private.

Redirecting his attention to his other brothers laughing and ribbing each other over who knew what, Neil had a strong feeling that an official announcement would be coming soon that Valerie would be their sister-in-law. His gaze darted from one brother to the other and he wondered which would be next to fall, because he knew as sure as he knew his name was Neil Francis Farraday that much sooner than later, another Oklahoma Farraday would join the ranks of the happily besotted Farradays.

MEET CHRIS

USA TODAY Bestselling Author of dozens of contemporary novels, including the award winning Aloha Series, Chris Keniston lives in suburban Dallas with her husband, two human children, and two canine children. Though she loves her puppies equally, she admits being especially attached to her German Shepherd rescue. After all, even dogs deserve a happily ever after.

More on Chris and all her books can be found at
www.chriskeniston.com

Follow Chris on Facebook at
ChrisKenistonAuthor

Never miss a New Release! Sign up for News from Chris:
www.chriskeniston.com/newsletter.html

Questions? Comments?
I would love to hear from you! You can reach me at:
chris@chriskeniston.com

CPSIA information can be obtained
at www.ICGtesting.com
Printed in the USA
BVHW030009090721
611458BV00005B/577